Jeremy kissed Jessica long and hard on the mouth. Clearly he felt like she was in his power and he could do whatever he wanted with her.

She tried her hardest to fake some enthusiasm, and Jeremy didn't seem to suspect anything. A moment later he drew back from her. "You stay right here and make yourself comfortable," he said huskily, placing heavy hands on her shoulders. "I'll be right back, and then . . ."

Jeremy disappeared downstairs. As soon as he was out of sight, Jessica leaped to her feet. Dashing to the window, she pushed the curtain aside and peered out into the snowy night.

Where are they? she wondered, panic slicing into her heart like a knife. Sam's car was nowhere in sight.

Jessica raced to the other side of the cabin. The same view met her eyes from that window. *Oh, no! They didn't make it.* The realization hit her like an avalanche. The whole time she'd been sitting on the couch with Jeremy, Jessica had felt protected by her knowledge that help was just a shout away. *I'm alone here,* Jessica thought, her teeth suddenly chattering. *They got lost or had an accident. I'm alone.*

A DEADLY CHRISTMAS

Written by
Kate William

Created by
FRANCINE PASCAL

BANTAM BOOKS
NEW YORK · TORONTO · LONDON · SYDNEY · AUCKLAND

RL 6, age 12 and up

A DEADLY CHRISTMAS

A Bantam Book / December 1994

Sweet Valley High® is a registered trademark of Francine Pascal
Conceived by Francine Pascal
Produced by Daniel Weiss Associates, Inc.
33 West 17th Street
New York, NY 10011
Cover art by Bruce Emmett

ISBN: 0-553-56629-6

Published simultaneously in the United States and Canada

Bantam Books are published by Bantam Books, a division of Bantam
Doubleday Dell Publishing Group, Inc. Its trademark, consisting of the
words "Bantam Books" and the portrayal of a rooster, is Registered in
U.S. Patent and Trademark Office and in other countries. Marca
Registrada. Bantam Books, 1540 Broadway, New York, New York 10036.

PRINTED IN THE UNITED STATES OF AMERICA

OPM   0 9 8 7 6 5 4 3 2 1

To Cassity Nicole Phillips

Chapter 1

Sixteen-year-old Jessica Wakefield sat on the edge of the family-room couch, her blue-green eyes glued to the TV screen in disbelief. "No," she whispered to herself. "It can't be."

Raising the remote control with a trembling hand, she hit the rewind button so she could watch the videotape one more time from the beginning.

Jessica herself had been wielding the camcorder she'd borrowed from her friend Amy Sutton just hours ago. The taped sequence was brief, but action packed. Jessica had started filming when Sue Gibbons, who had been kidnapped, appeared at the edge of the parking lot next to Glen's Grove gas station and convenience store. Even from a distance Sue looked bedraggled and frightened . . . understandably, since she'd just spent forty-eight hours tied up and gagged. Spotting Sue, Jessica's

1

twin sister Elizabeth had crossed the parking lot in order to place a briefcase full of money in a phone booth. Before she could even step out of the way, a man in a trench coat, hat, and dark glasses bolted past her into the booth to seize the ransom. As Elizabeth scurried off, the man quickly opened the briefcase. Apparently satisfied with its contents, he raced from the phone booth and disappeared behind the building.

Jessica rewound the tape again, just partway this time. She froze on the figure of the man emerging from the phone booth. In addition to the sunglasses and hat, a bandanna covered the lower part of his face; there was absolutely no way to identify him. At least that was what Jessica's family and Sam Diamond, the private investigator they'd hired to look into the kidnapping case, had concluded after viewing the tape.

Jessica licked her lips, which were dry as sandpaper, and glanced across the room. Her parents were talking quietly with Elizabeth; in the next room Jessica could hear the local police and Sam Diamond wrapping up their interviews with Sue about her harrowing experience. *None of them have a clue—I'm the only one who knows who he is,* she thought, gulping. *Ohmigod, how can this be happening?*

She forced her eyes back to the TV. She didn't want to believe what she saw with her own eyes, but there it was in living color. With the remote control, she'd frozen the kidnapper as he strode across the parking lot, the briefcase with six hundred thousand dollars in ransom money in his right hand. And on the little finger of his left hand, a gold ring glinted.

Another scene flashed into Jessica's mind. Just that afternoon she'd been sitting by the pool in her backyard with her fiancé, Jeremy Randall. Everyone in the family was on edge because of the kidnapping, but in the middle of all the tension and chaos, Jessica and Jeremy had been able to steal one perfect, idyllic moment. And in that moment she'd given him a ring as a token of her affection. It was one of the rings her older brother Steven had bought when he was engaged to his old girlfriend, Cara Walker—their plans to marry had fallen through, and Steven had hidden the rings in his desk drawer, where they'd waited for Jessica to find them.

The man's ring had been too small for Jeremy's fourth finger, so Jessica had slipped it onto his pinkie instead. She'd apologized for the poor fit, but he'd insisted it was perfect. "Because it's from you," he'd murmured as their lips met in a deeply passionate kiss.

The ring . . .

As Jessica stared in horror at the man in the video, it was as if the dark glasses, the hat, and the bandanna disappeared. She saw straight through the kidnapper's disguise . . . to the face of her beloved Jeremy.

3

Turning off the TV, Jessica buried her head in her hands. Her brain whirled, and she felt dizzy and nauseous. *It can't be. It doesn't make sense— none of it makes sense.* Then again, she asked herself, when was the last time anything *did* make sense?

She dimly remembered a time long ago when she was an ordinary high-school junior in Sweet Valley, California, hanging out at the Valley Mall and the beach, partying and gossiping with her friends. Everything was simple and uncomplicated; it felt like another lifetime. *It's like I've been in a fog ever since I got hit on the head with a Frisbee that day on the beach. . . .*

Leaning back limply against the couch, Jessica closed her eyes. The startling image on the TV screen was replaced by a wonderful picture: her first glimpse of gorgeous, sexy, sweet, exciting Jeremy Randall.

She'd been walking by the ocean with her best friend, Lila Fowler, when the Frisbee glanced off her forehead. The guy who'd thrown it hurried over to apologize to her, and with her first look at his tall, muscular, tanned body, his mane of shaggy golden hair, and his gold-flecked, coffee-brown eyes, Jessica had fallen head over heels in love. It was like a dream, really, or a scene from a movie. As Lila met and strolled off with Robby Goodman, the other Frisbee player, the blond Adonis had checked Jessica's pupils to make sure she didn't

4

have a concussion; he'd put an arm around her to support her, and suddenly they were kissing—a kiss like none Jessica had ever experienced. A lightning bolt of pleasure had torn through her body, but just as she started to lose herself in the sensation, he pulled away. "I can't see you ever again," he'd declared hoarsely, and disappeared before she could even learn his name.

The kiss had been unforgettable, and night and day Jessica found herself longing for her mystery man. Then, seemingly in answer to her prayers, he came knocking on her front door. That was when the dream temporarily turned into a nightmare.

As it happened, Jeremy Randall couldn't see Jessica again because he was engaged to another woman: Sue Gibbons, the Wakefields' houseguest. Sue was the only daughter of Alice Wakefield's beloved college roommate, Nancy, who had died just a short time earlier of a rare blood disease. When Sue wrote from New York that she and her fiancé, a fellow environmental activist working for the big conservation organization Project Nature, would love to have a California wedding, Alice had been delighted to invite her to Sweet Valley and help with the arrangements.

I tried to stay away from him, Jessica recalled, *but it was impossible. Our passion was like a tidal wave—unstoppable. How could I have let him marry another woman when he'd found true love with me?* For weeks Jessica and Jeremy had met

5

secretly, and finally Jeremy resolved to break off his engagement with Sue. Before he could, however, Sue floored Elizabeth, Jessica, and Jeremy with the announcement that she'd been diagnosed with the same disease that killed her mother. Most likely her own young life would be cut tragically short in a few years' time.

After the fact Sue confessed that she had lied about being ill; she was just desperately trying to hold on to Jeremy. But her ruse had had its desired effect, making Jeremy feel more obligated than ever to stand by her side. He'd go through with the wedding—he and Jessica would just have to sacrifice their happiness. Jessica had tried to accept this fate, but her love for Jeremy was too strong. As she stood on the beach at sunset, a bridesmaid in Sue and Jeremy's wedding, Jessica stared into the eyes of the groom and saw there a love that answered her own. She wasn't able to keep silent any longer. When the minister asked if anyone present knew a reason that this couple should not be bound in matrimony, Jessica's voice rang out loud and clear.

Now she almost laughed, remembering the chaos that ensued. Jeremy had admitted to all assembled that he was in love with Jessica, not Sue. A sobbing Sue was taken back to the Wakefields', and Jessica retreated to Lila's until the storm blew over. It never blew over completely, though—if anything it grew more violent with every passing day. Jeremy and Jessica became secretly engaged, but thanks to Lila soon everyone in Sweet Valley knew. When Jessica finally came home, Mr. and Mrs. Wakefield threatened boarding school for Jessica, and Sue attempted suicide by overdosing on sleeping pills. Jessica's parents forbade her to see Jeremy, but that didn't matter much since he was out of the country for a few weeks on business for Project Nature. Then came the fateful night of the Halloween costume party at Project Nature's mountain cabin. Jeremy was back in town, and Jessica was walking on air . . . until she spotted him in a clandestine embrace with none other than his ex-fiancée, Sue.

Jessica had left the party in tears, with Elizabeth at her heels. An hour or so later Jeremy had arrived at the Wakefields', but before Jessica could demand an explanation, he'd made the disturbing announcement: Sue had disappeared.

Sneaking out of the house, the twins had joined Jeremy in a late-night search of the woods surrounding the Project Nature cabin. They'd found Sue's gold locket, the chain broken. Their worst fears were confirmed the next morning when the Wakefields received a phone call demanding a large sum of money in exchange for Sue's safe return. She'd been kidnapped!

It all has something to do with the inheritance money, Jessica now surmised, trying to latch on to concrete details. She thought back to what she knew about Sue's inheritance. Having developed an intense dislike for her daughter's fiancé, whom she suspected of being a fortune hunter, Mrs. Gibbons had threatened to cut her daughter out of her will if Sue married Jeremy. True to her word, Nancy Gibbons willed her half-million-dollar fortune to Alice Wakefield instead. *Mom didn't find out until the day after Sue and Jeremy's canceled wedding, though,* Jessica mused, *and that's when we found out that the money would revert to Sue if she broke off contact with Jeremy for two months.* November 1 was the date on which Sue was to become an heiress; it was October 31 when Jessica spotted Sue and Jeremy together. Then Sue was abducted, and the kidnapper demanded the exact sum of Sue's inheritance as ransom.

OK, Jessica told herself, running her hands through her silky, shoulder-length blond hair. *Let's get this straight. Jeremy kidnapped Sue so he could steal her inheritance. Or maybe Sue wasn't "kidnapped" at all.* Jessica pondered this bizarre possibility. Sue's story was that she'd been tackled in the woods behind the cabin, then tied up, gagged, and blindfolded. "I was in a car—we were driving for what seemed like hours," Sue had told the police in a shaky voice. "When I got out of the car, it was cold, and I think there was snow on the ground. He kept me in a cold room—maybe an attic. But I never got a good look at him—I was blindfolded the whole time. . . ."

What if that's a lie? What if Sue and Jeremy

8

were in on it together? Jessica rubbed her eyes with her hands. That made even less sense. Why would Sue try to steal her own inheritance? Wasn't the money going to be hers anyway since she'd broken up with Jeremy? *Broken up with Jeremy* . . .

A flicker of doubt, sharp as a switchblade, pierced Jessica's heart. She remembered the momentary suspicion she'd had at a Sweet Valley High video-club meeting just a week or so ago. Winston Egbert had made a video about "The Best Places to Kiss in Sweet Valley," and Jessica could have sworn that she glimpsed Sue and Jeremy in the background of a misty, romantic beach shot. *Impossible,* she'd told herself at the time. *Jeremy's in Costa Rica. He and Sue broke up.* . . . Now she thought about seeing Sue and Jeremy together at the Halloween party. Jeremy had said Sue was making a last-ditch effort to reclaim his affection. When he resisted her advances, she'd broken down. He was just comforting her, there was nothing between them, there never had been, nothing like the feelings he had for Jessica. . . .

Jessica shook her head, amazed that she could have entertained such a traitorous thought for even one millisecond. Jeremy was the most honest, caring, adorable guy on the face of the planet . . . wasn't that why she was intending to spend the rest of her life with him? *He couldn't be the kidnapper, because he was here with us practically the whole*

9

time Sue was missing, Jessica reasoned. *In fact, he was standing right next to me when the kidnapper called to demand the ransom!* True, Sam Diamond claimed the ransom demands were taped in advance and then played over the phone, but so what?

Besides, Jeremy never cared about Sue's money, Jessica told herself. Mrs. Gibbons had been wrong about him; he'd been willing to take Sue even without a fortune. *Until he met me . . .*

The idea that Jeremy and Sue were in on this together somehow, that they were still in love, was the most ridiculous idea of all, Jessica decided. Jeremy had never *really* loved Sue—it was Jessica he was wild about. Jessica twisted the sapphire-and-diamond engagement ring around the fourth finger of her left hand, her eyes shining with renewed faith. *He loves me and I love him, and I trust him one hundred percent.*

"Sue, you're still shaking like a leaf," Alice Wakefield said, her voice warm with concern. She patted Sue's arm. "I'm going to make a pot of tea. Then we can get you in a hot tub and to bed."

"Thanks." Sue gave Mrs. Wakefield a tired, grateful smile. "I'll be fine now that I'm home, now that I'm safe."

Home . . . safe . . . As soon as Mrs. Wakefield headed toward the kitchen, Sue's smile faded, and an anxious frown took its place. She looked at her watch. *Nine o'clock . . . Jeremy was supposed to pick me up an hour ago. Where is he?* she wondered frantically.

Mr. Wakefield was at the front door saying good-bye to Sam Diamond and to Detective Belsky of the Sweet Valley police force. The twins were in the kitchen with their mother; Sue was alone. Quickly, she crossed the room and peered through the curtains into the dark night. Streetlights shone down on a handful of cars parked along Calico Drive, but none of them were Jeremy's.

Sue paced up and down in front of the window. She didn't understand what could have gone wrong. As they'd arranged, Sue had sneaked outside an hour ago to meet Jeremy, but he didn't show up. Not knowing what else to do, she'd returned to the house and further questioning by the police.

I think they believed my story, Sue thought, gnawing nervously on a fingernail. She'd stuttered a lot and almost started crying at one point, but that was to be expected from someone who'd just experienced the trauma of being kidnapped, right? Of course, it would have looked suspicious if she'd disappeared minutes after being released, and if Jeremy had never returned either. . . .

But it wouldn't have mattered, Sue reflected. *We would have been on our way to New York, and after tying up some loose ends, we would have*

11

taken off for Rio de Janeiro. It wouldn't even have
mattered that the ransom money turned out to be
fake. We would have found a way to survive. We'd
be starting a new life, we'd be putting the
Wakefields and Sweet Valley behind us forever. . . .

Alice and Ned Wakefield and their teenaged
daughter Elizabeth were some of the kindest people Sue had ever known, but all the same, she
couldn't help wishing she'd never met them. And
she might not have, if it hadn't been for Jeremy's
wild scheme. She remembered his reaction when
the will was read after her mother's death. He was
furious—she hadn't known he was capable of such
anger. Sue had been willing to choose love over
money, but Jeremy didn't see it that way. *He*
wanted us to have it all, love and money. But I
knew it was wrong from the start. Why did I go
along with any of it?

Sue looked around the Wakefields' family
room. It was a warm, lovely house, and she felt incredibly at home there. From the moment she arrived, Ned and Alice had treated her like a
daughter, and the twins had welcomed her as an
older sister. Tears of remorse stung Sue's eyes. It
had all been a lie, from the beginning. She and
Jeremy had come to Sweet Valley to plan a wedding that they never intended to go through with.
The whole point was for it to be called off, for
them to have a stormy breakup, for Jeremy to
enter a relationship with Jessica. Then, after two

months of estrangement, when the money reverted to Sue, she and Jeremy would leave Sweet Valley, quietly, separately. The Wakefields would never be the wiser.

But Jessica saw us together at the party. We were sure she'd tell, and the money would stay with Alice. We had to find another way to get it. . . .

Jeremy had come up with the kidnapping plan on the spur of the moment. The Halloween party had broken up. Before Sue could protest, Jeremy had hustled her into the drafty, dark attic of the Project Nature cabin and left her there with the spiders and bats. "We'll demand the exact amount of your inheritance as ransom," he'd declared, his eyes glinting. "It's only fair, Sue. It should be yours—ours. Don't you want what's coming to you?"

Now Sue clenched her hands into tight fists. *I should have refused. Faking a kidnapping . . . that was going too far.* But there was no arguing with Jeremy. He'd become obsessed with outwitting the Wakefields; he was willing to run any risk to get Sue's inheritance. *And what about me?* she wondered sadly. It had certainly started to seem as if he cared far more about the money than he did about her. When she'd summoned up the courage to tell him she wanted to call the whole thing off, he'd bullied her into submission, even taking the extreme measure of tying and gagging her "so it looks like the real thing, just in case someone finds you."

13

Sue rubbed her wrists together, remembering the cut of the rope on her flesh. How could a man do that to someone he loved? When she couldn't answer her own unspoken question, her throat tightened with more tears. *He doesn't love me anymore,* she thought, choking back a sob of despair. *Maybe he never loved me. Maybe Mom was right and it was just the money he wanted all along.*

She didn't want to believe it, but as the minutes ticked by, it became harder and harder to convince herself that Jeremy really was coming back for her. What if this had been his ultimate plan all along, to seize the money for himself and leave her behind? *It couldn't all have been lies,* Sue thought, remembering Jeremy's kisses and proclamations of love. *He lies about other things, but he couldn't lie about his feelings for me.* Even as she tried to convince herself of this, though, Sue knew she was hiding her head in the sand. Jeremy Randall had turned out to be ruthless, a consummate liar and actor driven to greater and greater extremes by his lust for wealth. If he could pretend to care for Jessica Wakefield, he could pretend to care for Sue Gibbons.

Sue stood at the window staring out into the dark, windy night and wondered how far Jeremy would get before he realized the money in the briefcase was fake. Would he think about returning to her, even for a moment, or had she lost her true love forever?

◦　　◦　　◦

14

"I think it's awfully strange that Jeremy hasn't shown up," Elizabeth said to Jessica as she squeezed a slice of lemon into her hot tea. "It's been hours. Why do you suppose he hasn't called?"

"I'm sure he—he probably—" Jessica sputtered. To her annoyance she couldn't think of a single plausible reason for Jeremy's behavior. "He'll be here, Liz. Just you—"

At that moment the doorbell rang. Elizabeth raised her eyebrows and muttered, "Saved by the bell." Her heart in her throat, Jessica raced from the kitchen into the front hallway.

Sue had bolted into the hallway, too. Stepping quickly in front of the other girl, Jessica grabbed the doorknob and yanked it open.

Jeremy Randall stood on the front step. He was wearing jeans, a red polo shirt, and a leather jacket. *No trench coat, no sunglasses, no hat, no bandanna,* Jessica thought, drinking in the handsome lines of his sun-bronzed, chiseled face. *Just Jeremy, wonderful Jeremy . . .*

His gold-flecked, deep-brown eyes burned into hers. As the powerful force of his love wrapped around her, Jessica wondered how she could ever have doubted it . . . or doubted him.

Jeremy scooped up Jessica in his arms and held her close against his broad, hard chest. "Thank God you're safe," he murmured, his voice husky with emotion. "I was so worried about you! Putting yourself in harm's way to drop off the ransom money . . . If anything had happened to you, I don't know what I'd—"

Their lips met in a fiercely sweet kiss. Jessica clung to him, her bones turning to jelly, as they did whenever she was in his arms. She was dimly aware of Sue standing in the background, witnessing this tender scene, and a feeling of satisfaction bubbled up inside her. Everyone, including Jeremy, had been worried sick about Sue for days. *Now it's my turn to get some attention,* Jessica thought happily.

Elizabeth stood at the other end of the hallway near the kitchen watching Jeremy and Jessica's reunion. *Nice of him to show up at last,* she thought sarcastically, her eyes narrowed. *He couldn't have been that worried about Jessica. I wonder where he's been all this time—it's close to midnight!*

Jeremy didn't offer an explanation for his absence, and Elizabeth figured that her starry-eyed twin wasn't about to demand one. Releasing Jessica, Jeremy turned to Sue. "Is it really you?" he exclaimed. "Are you all right? Did they hurt you?"

Jessica frowned as Jeremy bent forward to give Sue a brotherly hug. Patting Sue's back, Jeremy whispered something in her ear. Sue nodded, a smile warming her pale, tired face.

Now it was Elizabeth's turn to frown. She knew she should feel joyful and relieved that the whole terrible kidnapping episode was over. No one had

16

been hurt, Sue's inheritance remained intact, and sooner or later the police were bound to track down the kidnapper. But as she intercepted a look full of secret significance passing between Jeremy and Sue, Elizabeth realized that her stomach was still tied up in tense knots. *There's something really fishy about all of this. Something just isn't right. . . .*

Something . . . or someone. "Come have some tea, Sue," Mrs. Wakefield called from the kitchen. As Jeremy and Jessica retreated to the den and Sue disappeared into the kitchen, Elizabeth walked slowly up the stairs to get ready for bed. She knew the source of her discomfort was Jeremy. She'd disliked him from the start, when she realized he was two-timing Sue with Jessica. Now he was engaged to Jessica and supposedly through with Sue, but Elizabeth didn't trust him for a second. In Elizabeth's opinion, if Jeremy cheated on Sue, that meant he wouldn't hesitate to cheat on Jessica, either.

Of course, this wasn't the first time Elizabeth had disapproved of her twin sister's taste in guys. Jessica tended to focus on superficial things like looks, popularity, and wealth; if a boy drove a cool car, she could be persuaded to overlook any number of character flaws.

Not that I want to change Jessica, Elizabeth reminded herself. It would be so boring if she and Jessica were identical in personality as well as appearance! As it was, the resemblance stopped at the physical: underneath their sun-kissed blond hair, turquoise eyes, and slim, athletic figures, the twins were as different as avocados and artichokes. Elizabeth, the steady, "serious" twin, liked hanging out with the gang at the Beach Disco and the Dairi Burger, but she always gave homework and her journalism assignments for the school newspaper top priority. While Jessica was fickle and impetuous when it came to matters of the heart, Elizabeth drew great happiness and satisfaction from the fact that she and her boyfriend, Todd Wilkins, had weathered romantic storms to forge a relationship that would last.

Now the problem was that Jessica had settled down . . . but with the wrong guy. *He's much too old for her,* Elizabeth thought, *and he's just so slick—I really didn't believe him when he said he was just comforting Sue the other night at the Halloween party. Maybe I should have told Mom about that.*

She and Jessica had decided not to tell their parents that Sue had violated the agreement on which her inheritance hinged. Jessica at least felt satisfied with Jeremy's explanation, and then when they realized Sue had been kidnapped, it had seemed irrelevant. Now Elizabeth found herself wondering about it again. What was really going on Sunday night in the woods near the Project Nature cabin? Were Jeremy and Sue plotting something? What had Jeremy whispered to Sue just now, and where had he been the last hour or two?

The unanswered questions whirled madly in Elizabeth's head like falling leaves on an autumn wind. How did the kidnapper know the exact amount of Sue's inheritance, and how did he learn so quickly that the Wakefields had hired a private investigator? Why did the kidnapper communicate his ransom demands by playing pretaped messages over the phone? When he found out the money in the briefcase was fake, would he try again?

Elizabeth realized she was still too keyed up to fall asleep, and after changing into a flannel nightgown, bathrobe, and slippers, she padded back downstairs to the kitchen for a snack. She wasn't expecting to bump into anyone, having heard her parents and Sue go into their respective bedrooms, and assuming that Jessica and Jeremy had sneaked off someplace private to make out. When she entered the kitchen and saw the tall figure standing by the counter, she sucked in her breath in a startled gasp.

Jeremy turned to her, a genial smile creasing his movie-star-handsome face. "Sorry to scare you, Liz. We're all still a little on edge, eh?"

Elizabeth felt the hair stand up on the back of her neck. She didn't know how her sister could stand to be close to this guy; he gave her the heebie-jeebies. "I didn't know you were still here," she mumbled. "I just came down to . . . I think I'll be going back upstairs." She turned to leave.

"Stick around," said Jeremy. "I'm making hot chocolate for me and Jess—here, I'll pour you a cup."

Elizabeth shook her head. "That's OK." Jeremy's offer was nice enough, but she'd just as soon drink a cup of poison. "Thanks anyway," she said on her way out.

Jeremy was leaning against the counter, his hands in the back pockets of his jeans. "You don't like me, do you?" he called after her.

Elizabeth stopped in her tracks. She turned slowly, her cheeks burning. "I wouldn't exactly put it that way."

"Oh, come on." Jeremy's lips twisted, but whether in a smile or a sneer, Elizabeth couldn't tell. "You're usually honest to a fault, aren't you, Liz? So why don't you tell me to my face? What do you have against me?"

"OK, you want me to tell you, I'll tell you," Elizabeth burst out. "You're right, I *don't* like you. What you did to Sue was despicable. You have no values as far as I can tell—you're self-centered and manipulative, and you'll marry my sister over *my* dead body!"

Elizabeth braced herself for an angry retort. Instead, Jeremy laughed. "Do you really think you can control Jessica?"

"I don't have to control her," Elizabeth countered. "One of these days she'll come to her senses."

"I wouldn't count on it," drawled Jeremy. "She's

out of her mind over me, and she likes it that way."

Is he for real? Elizabeth wondered, repulsed by Jeremy's preening arrogance. "One thing's for sure, she could never think as highly of you as you do of yourself!"

"Listen to yourself," he said in a mocking tone. "Getting so worked up . . . I think you're a little jealous."

"Yeah, right!" Elizabeth sputtered.

"Admit it." He stepped closer to her, a sensual gleam in his eyes. "You're used to sharing everything with Jessica, but now she's left you way behind. Todd's just a kid—a safe bet. You wouldn't know what to do with a *real* man, would you, Liz?"

Angry words rushed to Elizabeth's lips, but she choked them back. *Todd Wilkins is one thousand times more of a man than you, you low-life jerk!*

But there was no point arguing with Jeremy. Nothing she said could offend him; he managed to twist everything into some kind of perverse compliment in his favor. "I think I'll pass on the hot chocolate," Elizabeth said rigidly. "Good night."

Jeremy smiled, plainly amused by her discomfort. "See you around, Elizabeth."

Still fuming, Elizabeth marched out of the kitchen with as much dignity as she could muster. Back in her room, she gave her pillow a couple of hard punches before climbing into bed. *When is Jessica going to wake up and tell that creep to take a hike?*

Chapter 2

"I can't believe that's why you weren't in school Monday and Tuesday!" Elizabeth's best friend, Enid Rollins, exclaimed.

It was Wednesday, and the Wakefield twins and a bunch of their friends were making the most of lunch period by eating outside in the sunny courtyard. While Aaron Dallas and Bill Chase tossed a Frisbee, Jessica and Elizabeth regaled the others with the tale of Sue's kidnapping and rescue.

"Sam Diamond—the private investigator—didn't want us to tell anyone what was going on," Elizabeth explained to Enid, leaning back on her elbows on the grass. "She was thinking about Sue's safety, and ours. But *somebody*"—Elizabeth nodded her head toward Jessica—"couldn't keep her big mouth shut!"

"What can I say?" Jessica smiled beguilingly.

"It was too good a story to keep to myself."

As she twisted the cap off a bottle of grapefruit juice, Lila Fowler picked up the narrative. "When I called on Monday to find out why she wasn't in school, Jessica started whispering all this top-secret stuff. I only heard part of it, but I would have sworn on my life that she said she and her family were being held for ransom!"

"So then Lila called me," Todd contributed between bites of his ham-and-Swiss sandwich. "And she, Robby, and I drove over to Liz and Jessica's to check out the situation."

"You looked in the windows, right?" said Jessica. "And you saw us all huddled together looking really worried and decided you had to come up with a plan to rescue us."

"And what a fine plan it was." Todd looked over at Lila, and she groaned. "A friend of Robby's who works for Sweet Valley Power got us a truck and uniforms, and we pretended to be maintenance men."

"Maintenance *people*," Lila corrected him, brushing a strand of silky brown hair over her shoulder.

"Right. We were going to get into the house on the pretense of checking some circuits or something and overpower the kidnappers," Todd concluded, "but needless to say, we had the story all wrong. We ended up tackling Jeremy and making total fools of ourselves!"

Winston, DeeDee, Enid, and the others all cracked up; Jessica also enjoyed the story immensely. In fact, the only person not laughing, Jessica noticed, was Elizabeth. *Typical Liz,* Jessica thought somewhat scornfully as she stirred up the fruit from the bottom of her carton of yogurt. *She's missing so much fun in life because she doesn't know when to stop worrying.* Luckily, Jessica didn't have that problem. Her worrying days were over. Pain-in-the-neck Sue was out of danger, so everything could get back to normal. Jessica smiled secretly to herself. *Back to normal? Make that back to heavenly. I have a date tonight. . . .*

"It's nice to be a family again," Alice Wakefield said to Sue on Wednesday evening as the Wakefields sat down to dinner. "It's so wonderful to have you back, I just can't tell you."

Mrs. Wakefield's voice was vibrant with emotion, and Elizabeth could see tears sparkling in her mother's eyes. *Mom would never have forgiven herself if any harm had come to Sue,* Elizabeth thought as she served herself some tossed green salad. Taking care of Sue was the last, best thing Mrs. Wakefield was able to do for her college friend Nancy. *But all's well that ends well, right?*

Sue pulled her chair closer to the table. "It's over. I just want to put it behind me."

"We all do," said Mr. Wakefield, his dark eyes solemn. "But I think we need to continue to be

24

careful. The kidnapper is still out there. Sam's following up on some leads in L.A., and the police are looking into the matter here—I'm sure it's just a matter of time before they run the kidnapper—or kidnappers—to ground. Of course, the easiest way to catch this guy would be if he tries to pass some of the counterfeit bills."

"I don't think he . . ." Sue stuttered to a stop. "I mean, won't he figure out that the money's fake?"

"I suppose that'll be the test," said Mr. Wakefield. "If he does, then maybe he's not such an amateur after all."

"Meanwhile, your inheritance is still safe and sound," Mrs. Wakefield assured Sue. "I talked to my accountant this morning, and a week from today the money will be transferred into your bank account in New York."

Sue's lips tightened; it almost looked to Elizabeth as if she were suppressing a smile. Elizabeth propped her elbows on the table and fixed Sue with her gaze. "So what are you going to do next, Sue?"

Sue blinked. "Oh, well, I haven't given it that much thought. I suppose I'll go back to New York eventually, and I'll look for a new job. After how things ended with Jeremy, I really don't have the heart to stay on with Project Nature."

Elizabeth opened her mouth to ask Sue another question and then shut it again. What was it about Sue that just didn't ring true? Why did Elizabeth have the persistent feeling that there was something wrong about Sue's "rightful" inheritance?

Her train of thought was interrupted when Jessica shoved back her chair and jumped to her feet. "I need to be excused," she announced. "The video-club meeting at Amy's starts in twenty minutes."

"But you didn't eat a bite," Mrs. Wakefield protested.

"They'll have food there," Jessica assured her. "I'm taking the Jeep—I won't be late."

Jessica hurried out of the dining room. A minute later Elizabeth patted her mouth with her napkin and then pushed back her own chair. "I'll be right back," she said, rising. "I just need to ask Jessica something about the video club. I'm thinking of joining myself, and . . ."

Letting her sentence trail off vaguely, she darted into the hallway and up the stairs. She found Jessica in her bedroom. In just a minute Jessica had changed from blue jeans and a cotton turtleneck into a clingy black tube miniskirt and a gauzy ruffled top with a deeply scooped neckline.

"Interesting choice for a video-club meeting," Elizabeth said, eyebrows raised.

Jessica turned her back on her sister. "Did you ever hear of knocking first?" she snapped.

"Your door was open."

"A knock would still be nice."

"Look, Jess, I know where you're going."

Elizabeth crossed the room so she could look her sister in the eye. "I think you should stay home."

"I have a video-club meeting," Jessica stated, "and if you have a problem with that, you can just—"

"Jessica," Elizabeth countered, "I'm your twin sister, remember? You don't belong to the video club. You're meeting Jeremy, and you know Mom and Dad would flip if they found out."

Jessica put her hands on her hips. "So why don't you turn me in?" she dared, her eyes flashing. "Go ahead, Liz. Snitch on me if it makes you feel better."

Elizabeth sat down on the edge of her sister's bed. "I don't want to snitch on you." She watched as Jessica stormed over to the full-length mirror and started brushing out her shimmering blond hair. "I want . . . I want you to see for yourself that Jeremy's not good for you."

Jessica shook her head in disbelief. "You don't know when to quit, do you, Liz?"

"I just don't trust him. I—"

Jessica whirled. "You don't have a single good reason not to like Jeremy," she cried, shaking the hairbrush at her sister. "How dare you judge him when you don't even really know him? You *don't* know him, Liz, not like I do. He *loves* me."

"You *think* he loves you, but that's what Sue thought, too, and look what happened to—"

"He loves me," Jessica repeated, visibly

struggling to contain her fury. "Case closed."

She turned her back again. With a sigh, Elizabeth drifted toward the bathroom that separated her bedroom from Jessica's. There was nothing she could do to stop her sister, short of ratting on her to their parents, and she wasn't about to stoop that low. *I have to let Jessica make her own mistakes, learn her own lessons,* Elizabeth thought. She shivered with apprehension. *I just hope she doesn't learn the hard way. . . .*

Jeremy raised his glass to Jessica, his eyes shining. "To the most beautiful, exciting girl in the world," he said, his voice husky, "who makes me the happiest guy in the world."

Jessica smiled, her cheeks flushed with pleasure. *If Liz could see us now!* she thought buoyantly.

Elizabeth just didn't know anything about real love, about *adult* love, Jessica decided as she stared raptly into Jeremy's eyes. Liz and Todd had a juvenile, high-school relationship—they simply hadn't scratched the surface of passion. Whereas Jessica and Jeremy . . .

At that moment Jessica didn't think she could possibly be happier. After telling her parents she was meeting the SVH video club at Amy's, she'd rushed to meet Jeremy at the Cypress Point Cafe, a tiny, secluded, very expensive, and indescribably romantic restaurant overlooking the surf in

Crescent Beach. When the maître d' had asked what name their reservation was under, Jeremy had given Jessica a secret wink and said, "Mr. and Mrs. Randall." Jessica had nearly fainted with ecstasy. One day in the not too distant future, after she graduated from high school and was eighteen, it would be true!

"I hope you like this place," Jeremy said now as the waiter set their entrées on the table. "I want this to be a special night."

Jessica took a tiny, delicate bite of her salmon en croûte. "It's perfect." She smiled, her dimple flashing. "Besides, Jeremy, *every* night with you is special."

"But I've been neglecting you lately." Jeremy's forehead wrinkled. "I was just so worried about Sue. I felt responsible somehow. But now that we know she's OK, and I have a break from Project Nature for a while, I can give all my attention to you."

Jessica's smile deepened. "I like the sound of that."

Reaching across the table, Jeremy took one of Jessica's hands in his. Her eyes were immediately drawn to the gold ring on his pinkie finger, and she almost laughed recalling her hysterical suspicion the previous night. "I just want to make sure you know how much you mean to me," Jeremy said. "Do you know?"

"I think so," Jessica whispered, her skin tingling from his touch.

29

"This should clear up any doubts." With his other hand Jeremy produced a long, flat jewelry box from an inside blazer pocket. "It's for you."

Her eyes bright with anticipation, Jessica lifted the lid of the box. A gold bracelet sparkling with tiny sapphires was nestled on the velvet inside. "Jeremy, it's breathtaking!" Jessica gasped.

"Then it's the right piece of jewelry for you. Here, allow me."

Jessica held out her arm so he could clasp the cool gold around her wrist. She stared at the bracelet, her face flushed with surprise and pleasure. Next to the sapphire-and-diamond engagement ring, this was the most beautiful gift anyone had ever given her. "I—I don't know what to say," she stammered.

"You don't have to say anything." Jeremy's lips curved in an unbelievably sexy smile. "Just enjoy it."

The rest of the meal passed in a blur. Jessica was too excited to do more than pick at her salmon; as always, being with Jeremy took away her appetite for everything but him.

"It's a beautiful night—let's take a walk on the beach," Jeremy suggested as they left the restaurant. "I think there's a path over here."

Hand in hand, they followed the cobblestone path to the edge of a grassy dune. Ahead of them, waves crashed against the shore, the surf foaming silver in the moonlight.

As they stepped onto the cool sand, Jessica shivered. Quickly, Jeremy wrapped his arms around her. "Are you cold?" he asked. "Here, let me warm you up. . . ."

He touched his lips to hers in a lingering, leisurely kiss. Gradually, the kiss grew deeper, more urgent, until Jessica felt as if her whole body were on fire. She twined her arms around his neck and pressed against him, wishing they could stay joined like this forever and ever and ever. . . .

"Jessica," Jeremy whispered, his lips traveling along her jawline and then down her throat.

"Hmm," she murmured.

He pushed the collar of her blouse aside, and she felt his lips warm against the bare skin of her shoulder. "That bracelet is just a little token—it doesn't begin to show the depth of my feelings for you. What I feel is so strong. . . . I just don't know if I can wait until our wedding night to show you how much I love you."

He pulled her close. They were kissing again, making Jessica feel dizzy and weak. "Oh, Jeremy," she whispered. "Are you saying what I think you're . . ."

"I want us to be together, *really* together. I want us to belong to each other, body and soul."

"Oh, Jeremy . . ."

"Friday night," he murmured. "I'll scout out the perfect romantic hideaway for us, and then . . ."

31

"Oh, Jeremy," Sue whispered, wrapping her arms around him and hugging him tight. "I'm so glad we finally have some time alone together."

When Jeremy had walked through the Wakefields' front door the night before, all Sue's doubts and worries had disappeared like mist before the rising sun. Even as he embraced Jessica, he'd met Sue's eyes, and then when it was her turn, he'd whispered in her ear, "The money's fake. We'll have to hold tight for a few more days. . . ."

Now it was late Wednesday evening. After parting from Jessica, Jeremy had phoned Sue from the room he'd rented, and she'd agreed to sneak into the backyard after the rest of the family had gone to bed. They were lying in the hammock, which was shielded from view of the house by the fronds of a palm tree.

Jeremy stroked Sue's hair, and she buried her face against his chest. "I don't know how I'd live without you," she said softly. "Now that Mom's gone, I have no one—I'd be so alone if it weren't for you. Oh, I love you so much."

"I love you, too." Jeremy pressed a tender kiss on Sue's forehead. "And you don't have to worry about being alone. I'll take care of you, Sue, I promise."

"At the cabin . . . I was afraid," she confessed. "I was afraid you didn't love me anymore."

"I was rough with you," Jeremy admitted remorsefully. "I'm so sorry. I was just so incredibly tense—I didn't want anything to go wrong. Can you forgive me?"

"Of course, if you'll forgive me for freaking out on you the way I did. When I said I wanted to back out . . . I just lost my head for a minute."

He gave her an encouraging squeeze. "Then you're still with me?"

"Body and soul," she promised. "It's all going to be OK, isn't it? We can do this without hurting the Wakefields."

"You bet," Jeremy said breezily. "Next week the money will be yours fair and square. We'll hang around for a few days so that no one gets suspicious. Then you'll fly back to New York—supposedly alone—and I'll leave on a Project Nature 'business trip.' But really it'll be you and me and half a million dollars in a tropical paradise—what a life!"

Sue sighed. "I just wish we could've known the twins wouldn't say anything about seeing us together the night of the Halloween party. The whole kidnapping scheme wasn't really necessary, was it? And now they're hunting for you. What if—"

Jeremy put a finger to her lips. "They can hunt all they like, but they won't find me," he said with supreme self-confidence.

"I'll tell you what I hate," said Sue, pretending to pout. "I hate the idea of your spending one more minute with Jessica Wakefield. I can't wait to get out of Sweet Valley and have you all to myself again!"

Jeremy chuckled. "The only reason I'm hanging out with Jessica is that it was a foolproof way to break up the wedding and get your money back."

A lingering doubt prodded Sue. "You don't like her . . . even a little bit?"

"Jessica?" Jeremy scoffed. "She's a bore—a complete child and totally unsophisticated. But, then, no girl could hold any charms for me compared to you."

Before Sue could ask any more questions, Jeremy's lips pressed down on hers in a fiery, possessive kiss. Sue gave herself up to the joy of feeling safe and warm in his strong arms. *He does love me and me alone,* she assured herself. *We're going to have a happy ending, just like in the fairy tales. . . .*

"Save tomorrow night just for me?" she pleaded.

"I have to see Jessica on Friday," Jeremy told her, "but tomorrow night, sure. I'll be all yours."

Jessica lay on her bed in the dark, her eyes wide open and her heart racing. As she stared at the moon shadows dancing on the ceiling, Jeremy's words echoed in her feverish brain. "I don't know if I can wait until our wedding night to show you how much I love you. . . ."

A tingly shiver chased up and down Jessica's

body, and she kicked her feet under the covers, smiling to herself. "To belong to each other, body and soul," she whispered to herself, quoting Jeremy. What would it be like to be with him like that, to go all the way?

I'm scared to find out, but I'm dying to. I'm ready . . . no I'm not . . . yes, I am. . . .

Jessica debated with herself in delicious torment. She'd never gotten in this deep with a guy before; none of her other relationships, even with Sam Woodruff, had been this serious. *Maybe it's time*, she thought, picturing Jeremy's intense brown eyes, glowing with love and desire. *I'm sixteen—I'm old enough to make a mature decision about this.* That it was a momentous decision, Jessica had no doubt. But she also had no doubt that her feelings for Jeremy were real. They had a one-of-a-kind love that was never going to die.

Jessica imagined Jeremy lying in the bed next to her and shivered again. What would it be like?

He can't wait to find out, and neither can I, she realized, hugging her pillow tightly. *And why should we wait? We're madly in love, and we're practically married already.* She twisted the engagement ring on her finger. *I'm old enough, and it's the right thing to do. After all, I'm an engaged woman. . . .*

Jeremy watched Sue run lightly across the backyard, a ghostly figure in her pale nightgown and robe. The sliding glass door closed behind her soundlessly, and she was gone.

His hands in his jeans pockets, he strode around the side of the Wakefields' house and down the sidewalk to where he'd parked his car half a block away. He couldn't wait to get back to the room he rented and go to sleep—it had been an exhausting evening.

But a fun one, too, he thought with a sly smile. On the one hand, he was frustrated and irritated by the roadblocks that kept interfering with his plans. One thing after another kept going wrong. He would have been on an island in the South Pacific by now if the ransom money hadn't been fake, but when he figured that out—and he was an expert, it didn't take long—he'd hurried back to the Wakefields to reestablish his innocence, instead of deserting Sue as he'd intended. But the one-way plane ticket was still tucked safely away, and he'd come up with another strategy. *The money's being transferred into her New York bank account electronically. . . . There are all sorts of things you can do with computers these days, if you're smart and ready to run a few risks. . . .*

He licked his lips, anticipating. Soon he'd have Sue's inheritance, every penny of it . . . without Sue. He didn't plan to share the money and never had. *Patience,* he said to himself, just as he'd said to Sue earlier. *A week from Saturday, you'll be out of here. . . .*

In the meantime . . . He thought about Jessica, the night wind whipping her long blond hair, and her innocent blue-green eyes wide with love and trust. All he had to do was whisper a few lovey-dovey words, ply her with jewelry bought on credit—by the time the creditors came after Jeremy Randall, he'd no longer exist—and she was putty in his hands, just like Sue. *I have ten days to kill, so I might as well enjoy myself,* Jeremy thought. *Might as well get some kicks along the way. . . .*

Chapter 3

"I was just making fruit-and-yogurt parfaits for Jessica and me," Elizabeth said as Sue wandered into the kitchen on Thursday morning. "Want one?"

Sue shook her head, stretching. "Is there any hot coffee? I could use a jump start."

Elizabeth poured a mug of coffee for Sue and then carried the yogurt parfaits and a box of granola over to the kitchen table. "You look tired," she commented to Sue. "Are you having trouble sleeping?"

An odd smile flitted briefly across Sue's face. Then she hugged herself, shivering. "Yeah, I guess I am. I'm trying to forget about the kidnapping, but it's haunting me. Especially at night."

Jessica yawned widely. "I'm tired, too," she declared, winking at Elizabeth. "I was awake all night thinking about how much fun I had at the video-club meeting."

Sue intercepted the frown Elizabeth directed at her twin. "Jessica, were you out with Jeremy last night?" she asked.

Jessica raised her eyebrows haughtily. "And what business of yours would that be?"

"I don't want to butt in, but I care about you, Jessica. You and Liz are like sisters to me—I don't want to see you hurt the way I was."

"Well, Sue, I hate to be the one to break it to you, but it's going to be different for Jeremy and me from the way it was for the two of you," Jessica declared, lifting her spoon. "He'd never hurt me— he loves me."

"That's what *you* think. Jeremy's a two-timer. He'll just use you until someone new comes along, and then he'll drop you like a stone the way he dropped me." Suddenly Sue, who had always been superficially polite to Jessica on the subject of Jeremy, appeared to be boiling with anger and bitterness. "Just thinking about him makes me ill. I don't want to lay eyes on him ever again. Take my advice, Jessica—break the engagement before he breaks it for you."

"If you feel that way, Sue, why don't you go back to New York?" Pushing back her chair, Jessica stood up to carry her bowl to the sink. "It's been nice chatting with you," she said, her voice dripping with sarcasm and disdain. "Thanks for the sisterly concern. Have a nice day."

"I didn't mean to tick her off," Sue said to

Elizabeth after Jessica left the room. "But I really do think she'd be better off getting Jeremy out of her life."

"Hmm, definitely," Elizabeth agreed. Crunching a spoonful of granola, she studied Sue thoughtfully. She was a little surprised by Sue's vehemence—it was a big switch to hear her talk so negatively about Jeremy. *Then again, maybe I shouldn't be surprised,* Elizabeth mused. Sue was totally unpredictable and emotional. *Maybe she's just jealous, like Jessica thinks. Or maybe . . .* Elizabeth recalled Jeremy's story about what happened at the Project Nature Halloween party. "Sue just threw herself at me. I can't seem to make her see that it's over between us. . . ."

Sue had been through a lot of terrible things, and Elizabeth felt sorry for her, but at the same time, she couldn't shake the impression that Sue wasn't being entirely open and honest. *What's up with her? What kind of game is she playing?*

"I'll say one thing for Jeremy," Elizabeth offered. "He was really frantic while you were missing, and ready to do anything to get you back safely."

"Well, he—I guess he still cares about me just a little."

"We were all fearing the worst," said Elizabeth. "It must have been horrible, being tied up and blindfolded."

"It was," confirmed Sue, wrapping both hands around the mug of steaming coffee.

"But you put up a pretty good fight. Your necklace was ripped off, right?"

"My necklace?" Sue looked puzzled. "Oh, right—he grabbed me by the throat and hurled me down. That must have been how it happened. Oh, Liz, let's not talk about this anymore." She lifted her mug. "I need a refill. Can I pour you one?"

"No, thanks."

Elizabeth watched Sue pour herself another cup of coffee. Instead of sitting down again, Sue moved toward the door. "I think I'll go back to bed. I'm still feeling a little tired and shaky."

"Sorry for dredging up that scary stuff," Elizabeth said. "Take it easy, OK?"

Alone in the kitchen, Elizabeth finished her breakfast, then rinsed out the bowl and put it in the dishwasher, all the while mulling over her conversation with Sue. *I can't put my finger on it, but something's not right*, she decided. *She doesn't seem that sure of her story—why is that? Is it because it was so upsetting, she gets flustered talking about it, or is there another reason?*

The whole web was so tangled. Sue and Jeremy, Jeremy and Jessica . . . and in the middle of the web, Sue's half-million-dollar inheritance. *People go to all sorts of extremes when that kind of money's at stake,* Elizabeth reflected. The other night Sam Diamond had hinted that she was onto something—or someone—but they hadn't heard

41

from her in a few days. *I wonder . . . is this web even more twisted than it appears?*

Jessica floated down the hall between classes at Sweet Valley High, a dreamy, distracted smile on her face. *Tomorrow night, Jeremy's going to show me how much he loves me. . . . Wow, what am I going to wear?*

She knew there were practical, serious things to consider, like birth control. No matter how much she loved Jeremy, Jessica knew she still had to protect herself from pregnancy and sexually transmitted diseases. She'd be sure to take care of that—it would be easy enough to buy condoms at the drugstore—but in the meantime, she wanted to think about the more romantic aspects of the proposed rendezvous. *We'll have candles, and maybe a bottle of wine. Soft music playing in the background: classical? No, that would be too fancy and formal—I wouldn't feel like myself. Whitney Houston—that's it. I'll slip into the bathroom to change into something more comfortable, and then . . .*

"Ouch!" Jessica yelped, her fantasy disrupted.

Rounding a corner in the hallway, she'd walked right into Ken Matthews, Sweet Valley High's star quarterback and one of her good friends. "Sorry, Jess," Ken said, steadying her with his strong, sure hands. "Didn't mean to run you over. Are you all right?"

Jessica rubbed her arm, making a pretend face of pain. "We're not on the football field, you know," she kidded. "Do I look like an opposing lineman or something?"

Ken laughed. "Hardly. In fact"—his handsome face flushed slightly—"you look really pretty today. That's a nice dress."

Jessica glanced down at her red knit T-shirt dress. It was one of her oldest outfits and totally plain; she'd been too busy thinking about tomorrow night to care about how she looked going to school—after all, she wasn't going to bump into Jeremy at SVH, and she was saving her sex appeal for him. "Thanks. Well, I'll see ya," she said, continuing down the hall.

"'Bye, Jess," Ken called after her.

Now where was I? Jessica thought. *Oh, that's right. I've slipped into something more comfortable—Jeremy's lit a fire in the fireplace—and then . . .*

"So I expect you all to volunteer to be on one of the committees for the Mistletoe Madness dance," Pamela Robertson informed her friends at lunch on Thursday. Pamela and her boyfriend Bruce Patman were the cochairs of this year's holiday dance, scheduled for a week from Friday. "Amy, you said you'd help with decorations, right?"

Tucking a strand of long, ash-blond hair behind her ear, Amy Sutton nodded. "Sure, and I think I

43

can talk Barry into helping, too." She smiled mischievously. "We'll have fun hanging the mistletoe."

"What about you, Lila?" Pamela asked. "Which committee do you want to be on: refreshments, decorations, music?"

"Sorry," said Lila, squeezing a packet of low-cal dressing onto her chef's salad. "You know manual labor isn't my thing—I'm just not the committee type."

"Well, how about publicity?" Pamela pressed. "You could design the posters—Robby could help."

"That's right, Robby's a painter," said Winston. "Doesn't he have an art opening coming up?"

Lila pursed her lips. She'd met eighteen-year-old Robby Goodman on the beach the very same day Jessica had met Jeremy Randall; they'd hit it off immediately and had been dating for a few months now. Lila was crazy about him—in fact, she'd never been quite so serious about a boy before. Maybe he hadn't turned out to be rich as he'd pretended when they first met, but Robby had a lot of natural sophistication and style; he was smart, talented, interesting, funny, sweet, and drop-dead gorgeous. There was only one problem. . . .

"The gallery's mounting an exhibit of local artists," Lila confirmed. "It opens next Wednesday. But I have to say, I'm kind of worried. As far as I can tell from snooping around his studio, he hasn't produced a single painting, and time's running out."

Winston gestured carelessly. "He's probably just overextended—you made him sign up for that business course at the university, right? I'm sure he'll throw something together."

"He has to do better than that, though," said Lila. "This is his first big opening—it could make or break his career."

Amy snapped the top on a can of lemon-flavored seltzer. "Are you really surprised that he's disorganized, Li? I mean, if you ask me, this sounds like vintage Robby."

Lila narrowed her brown eyes at Amy. "What do you mean?"

"Robby's not exactly a go-getter—he wouldn't be taking that class if you hadn't made him. He's post-poning college, living with his dad, puttering around the studio . . . if you ask me, that's what he's going to be doing for the rest of his life." Amy, a hotline volunteer at the local youth center, was clearly getting into her psychoanalysis of Robby. "He has a fear of success or something—he's never going to make a name for himself. What's surprising is that you haven't lost your patience with him long before now."

"Amy, you are so off base it's not even funny," Lila exclaimed. She tossed her mane of long, silky hair, her face bright with fury. "Obviously you don't know anything about the artistic temperament. For your information, Robby . . ."

Lila's sentence trailed off. For the life of her, she couldn't think of one thing to say in Robby's defense.

At that moment someone stepped up behind Lila and tapped her shoulder. "Hey, Li," Jessica hissed in her ear. "I need to talk to you for a sec. Alone."

Lila was relieved to have an excuse to terminate the conversation about Robby. She trotted after Jessica to a secluded corner table. "What's up?" she asked, her curiosity piqued by her friend's air of mystery.

"I need to ask you for a *big* favor," said Jessica, holding her hands wide to indicate the magnitude. "You've got to go shopping with me tonight."

"I thought after your last charge at Bibi's you were forbidden to set foot in the mall until after the turn of the new millennium," Lila replied dryly.

"That's why I need you. I'm a little short on cash, and Mom won't let me use her charge card—"

"That's never stopped you before," Lila pointed out.

"And besides," Jessica continued, ignoring the interruption, "I don't want my parents to know what I'm buying."

"What *are* you planning to buy?"

Jessica gave Lila a sphinxlike smile. "You'll see."

"C'mon, tell me. Is it clothes? Something else?"

Jessica shook her head, her eyes twinkling. "If you come with me to the mall and give me a loan, you'll find out tonight," she promised.

"Jessica, you're a real pain," said Lila, but she

was too intrigued to say no. "OK, I'll lend you the cash—at the prime rate plus one."

Jessica stuck out her tongue. "Boy, are you stingy!"

Lila grinned. "You've got to respect money if you want to have a lot of it!"

"I just can't figure Sue out," Elizabeth said to Todd as she walked him to basketball practice after school. "Now she's acting like she hates Jeremy."

"It's understandable—the guy ditched her at the altar," Todd pointed out.

"True," Elizabeth conceded. "But then there's the whole kidnapping thing. Sometimes she seems totally traumatized by it—her teeth chatter, she's practically in tears, whatever. Other times she acts like it wasn't that big a deal. She's relaxed, casual, businesslike, and ready to make plans to go back to New York and resume her life. She's like a split personality or something."

"She's a pretty mixed-up girl," Todd concluded. "But we've known that for a while."

Elizabeth sighed. "I like her, I really do. But I don't *know* her. I thought I did, but lately I keep getting the feeling when we talk that she's putting on an act. Something's going on under the surface, but she won't let me see what it is."

Todd slung his arm around Elizabeth's shoulders and gave her a squeeze. "You've been a good friend to Sue. That's probably the most you can do for her."

"But I haven't helped solve the mystery behind her kidnapping," Elizabeth said with a sigh.

"That mystery may never be solved. But here's a mystery I bet we can clear up right away," he said, his tone playful. "Who should I take to the Mistletoe Madness dance?"

"Oh, you . . ."

Stepping to the side of the corridor, Todd leaned against the wall and pulled Elizabeth close for a long kiss. "So do we have a date?" he murmured.

She nodded, too busy kissing him back to reply.

Outside the boys' locker room, they made another date to meet later that afternoon—Elizabeth was getting a ride with Todd because Jessica had the Jeep. As she strolled on toward the newspaper office, Elizabeth couldn't help smiling to herself. The sweetness and security of her and Todd's relationship was so special. Her smile faded. Jessica thought she'd found the same thing with Jeremy . . . but had she?

The *Oracle* office was crowded; Mr. Collins, a popular English teacher and the newspaper's adviser, had called a special staff meeting. He waved to Elizabeth as she took a seat next to her friend Olivia Davidson, the paper's arts editor, and then clapped his hands together. "I've got big news for you folks," he announced. "As of today our computers are on-line with INFOMAX."

The room exploded into cheers. "Can we really

use it to access newspaper files all over the country?" asked John Pfeifer, the sports editor.

"Any paper, big or small," Mr. Collins confirmed. "Here, let me show you how it works."

He pulled up a chair in front of one of the computer terminals. His hands moved quickly over the keyboard. "There are a couple of ways to get at information. You can check the index for a particular newspaper, or you can research by topic. For example, we could reference every article that's been written recently about NAFTA, the North American Free Trade Agreement."

Oracle editor in chief Penny Ayala laughed. "That would be a pretty long list."

"You're not kidding." Mr. Collins grinned at Penny. "What do you think we'll find if we type in . . ."

Looking over Mr. Collins's shoulder, Elizabeth watched him type out Penny's name. She gasped as a list of newspaper articles flashed on the screen. "Look, Penny!" Elizabeth cried. "It's about you!"

"These are all the news stories where Penny's name is mentioned," said Mr. Collins. "A dozen or so *Oracle* articles and even a couple in the *Sweet Valley News*. By clicking on any one, you can bring up the text on the screen."

"This is the coolest," said staff writer and photographer Allen Walters. "We could find out anything about anyone!"

Elizabeth stared at the bright, blinking computer screen, an idea fizzing to life in her brain. All at once she had an experiment she couldn't wait to try out. . . .

Fifteen minutes later the meeting broke up, with Penny, Allen, and the others either heading home or settling down to work. Taking a seat at a vacant computer terminal, Elizabeth quickly accessed INFOMAX and typed in the name "Jeremy Randall." She held her breath as the program searched all the available files for any reference to Jeremy. What might she discover?

Only two references? Elizabeth thought a moment later. She clicked on the first one, which turned out to be a story covering Project Nature activities that had appeared recently in a New York City newspaper. The second article was the announcement of Jeremy's engagement to Sue as printed in the *Sweet Valley News*.

So much for finding something juicy. Elizabeth heaved a sigh of disappointment. She supposed she shouldn't be surprised—if anything incriminating were out there, Sam Diamond would have dug it up by now.

Still, it was odd. Elizabeth drummed her fingers on the table, frowning. Penny Ayala, who was only sixteen, appeared in a fairly long list of articles, while there were only two about twenty-three-year-old Jeremy, both dated within the past six months. *Strange,* Elizabeth thought. *I'm trying to find out about Jeremy's past, but it's almost like he doesn't have one.* A chill chased up her spine. She wanted to be able to pin something on Jeremy Randall; she wanted to figure out who he was, what he was after. But she couldn't get a handle on him—he kept slipping through her fingers. It was almost as if Jeremy Randall had materialized out of thin air.

Chapter 4

Jessica, Amy, Maria, and the other Sweet Valley High cheerleaders stood in a circle on the athletic field arguing about changes to one of their routines. "I still think we should do a back crunch instead of a spread eagle," said Jessica's cocaptain, Robin Wilson. "And a round-off back-handspring combination is always a peppier way to start out than a—"

"Fine, whatever," interrupted Jessica, tapping her foot impatiently. "I don't really care how we do it. See you guys tomorrow, OK?"

"Where are you off to in such a hurry?" called Amy as Jessica bent to grab her sweatshirt and book bag from the bench and then took off in the direction of the student parking lot.

"I have an important errand to run," Jessica shouted back.

Jingling the keys to the Jeep in her hand,

Jessica smiled to herself as she sauntered along. *Boy, is Lila going to flip when she finds out we're going shopping for garters and teddies!* she anticipated.

A steady stream of students flowed from the gym to the parking lot; extracurricular activities and sports-team practices were wrapping up. As Jessica approached the Jeep, she saw a tall, well-built blond guy jogging toward her. Ken waved and Jessica stopped to wait for him.

"Hey, what's up?" she said.

"Oh, nothing much. Just wanted to say hi."

Jessica smiled at Ken, an inquiring look on her face. She got the feeling he wanted to talk to her about something. Instead of moving on to his car, he just stood there, shuffling his feet and looking down at the pavement. *What's with Ken, the superjock?* she wondered. He wasn't the type to get tongue-tied talking to a girl, especially a girl he'd known for a million years, like her. "Spit it out, Matthews," she prompted genially.

"Oh, it's nothing, I just . . ." To her surprise red blotches spotted Ken's face. "I know you're probably busy, but the gang is meeting at the Dairi Burger after the football game tomorrow night, and I was wondering if . . ." He looked up and met her eyes, smiling sheepishly. "We haven't seen you much lately, you know? I mean, you're never around, being engaged and all. I—the whole gang, we kind of, um, miss you."

"The game—shoot, that's right," said Jessica. She'd have to cheer and then rush straight home to get ready for her big date. "Thanks for thinking of me, Ken, but yeah, I do have plans already. Pretty important plans," she added, blushing herself as she thought about Jeremy. "See you tomorrow, OK?"

Jumping into the Jeep, she revved the engine, rolling down the window as she did so. Ken stepped aside as she backed out of the parking space. "So long, Jess."

Lifting her hand carelessly in reply, Jessica screeched off, leaving him behind in a cloud of dust.

Lila checked the clock on the dashboard of her green Triumph as she coasted out of the long, winding driveway of Fowler Crest, her family's palatial home on Country Club Drive in the exclusive hill section of Sweet Valley. She had half an hour before she had to meet Jessica at the Valley Mall. There was plenty of time to swing by Robby's first.

Her boyfriend lived with his father in the carriage house of a large estate with a sweeping, dramatic view of the Pacific. Lila knocked on the door; when no one answered, she turned the knob and let herself in. "Hello? Anybody home? Robby?"

Robby appeared at the top of the stairway, a smile of surprise on his face. He'd set up a studio under the eaves on the second floor. *And that's where he's been,* Lila deduced. *That's a good sign, anyway!*

"Look at you," Lila teased as Robby hurried across the room to greet her with a hug. "That shirt is covered with paint. Ugh, don't get it on me!"

"It's old and dry," he assured her. "I'm just doing some sketching today."

"Just some sketching?" Her smile faded. "Well . . . can I see what you're working on?"

He shrugged. "Sure, come on up."

Lila followed Robby up the staircase. Stepping into the sunny studio, she raked it with her eyes. Just like the last time she'd stopped by, she saw nothing but a stack of blank canvases leaning against the wall and a drafting table littered with charcoal sketches.

"See?" Robby held up one of the drawings. "I'm working out the composition for a painting of the Sweet Valley Marina."

Lila eyed the drawing. It didn't look like much—just a jumble of boats and piers, nothing that could be hung in a gallery, that was for sure. "Is that going to turn into a painting?" she asked skeptically.

"One of these days," Robby asserted cheerfully.

"Will it be done in time for the opening?"

He shrugged again. "Maybe."

Until now Lila had refrained from bugging Robby about the progress of his painting. When she registered him for the business course without his knowledge, he'd gotten pretty mad, and she'd vowed not to be so bossy. She couldn't try to change Robby; she had to love him for who he was. But now she couldn't keep silent any longer. "So where are the paintings you *are* planning to exhibit? Can I see them?"

Robby dropped his eyes. He kicked at a pencil that had fallen on the floor and then looked up again, directing his gaze not at Lila but at an empty easel standing on the other side of the room. "Actually . . ." he mumbled, running a hand nervously through his rumpled dark hair. "To tell you the truth, Li . . . I haven't finished any of the paintings for the show yet."

Her jaw dropped. This was even worse than she had expected. "Not *one*? But the show's in less than a week!"

"I'm not worried," he said, shooting her a disarming smile. "Why should you be?"

"Because the invitations have already gone out, and it's too late for you to back down," she declared, shaking her head in exasperation. "Because your career's on the line."

Robby raised his eyebrows. "Li, I said you don't need to worry. I'll throw something together by Tuesday."

"You'll throw something together—do you really think that's . . ." Lila bit her tongue.

"Hey." Robby stepped toward her, his arms outstretched. After a moment's hesitation Lila leaned into him for the hug. "Don't you have faith in me?" he asked, his lips against her hair.

Lila nodded. "Of course I do," she said, glad that her face was pressed against his chest and he couldn't see her expression. Because as much as she loved him, she wasn't sure she *did* have faith in him. Amy had really ticked her off, but Lila couldn't help feeling that maybe her friend had struck on the truth. Was Robby a washout?

"Let's check out the Unique Boutique," Jessica said as she and Lila forged into the crowded Sweet Valley Mall late Thursday afternoon.

"Don't you like Bibi's and Lisette's better for dresses, though?" asked Lila. "The Unique Boutique has mostly bathing suits and lingerie and . . ." Lila stopped in her tracks and put her hands on her hips. Jessica grinned at her. "Jessica Wakefield, exactly what are we shopping for?"

"Something to go with my beautiful new bracelet," Jessica said, dangling her bejeweled wrist in front of Lila's eyes. "C'mon and you'll see."

On the way to the Unique Boutique, Lila told Jessica about her most recent visit with Robby. "He could be on the verge of making a major fool of himself," she bemoaned. "I mean, if this show opens and people—we're talking, like, *major* art critics—show up from all over the place to check out his work and he doesn't have anything to hang on the wall, how will it look?"

"Crummy," said Jessica.

"I mean, it's OK to put off college and live at home for a while after you graduate from high school." Lila wrinkled her nose. "I personally wouldn't want to do it, but it's OK if you've got a reason, if you're accomplishing some goal or other. But if Robby's doing it so he can be an artist, and he's not even *painting* . . ."

"What's really bugging you?" asked Jessica. "Is it that Robby's not painting or that Amy and Caroline were giving you a hard time at lunch about his being a loser?"

Lila chewed what little color was left off her lips, then reached into her pocketbook for a lipstick. "A little of both, I guess."

"If he's not the guy you thought he was, blow him off."

"But I'm in love with him!" Lila burst out.

Jessica laughed. "Then stop paying attention to what other people say. Follow your heart." Her eyes misted over with a dreamy fog. "People all over the place have been trying to break up me and Jeremy, but we care too much for each other to let them get in our way. Don't give up on Robby, Li—fight for this."

Lila nodded her head with new determination. "Alright, I will." She squeezed Jessica's arm. "Thanks, Jess."

Entering the Unique Boutique, Jessica led Lila straight to the lingerie section. "They have a lot of sexy stuff here," Lila observed, fingering a red silk teddy.

"Then I'm bound to find what I'm looking for," said Jessica. Taking the teddy from the rack, she held it against her body and turned to Lila. "What do you think?"

Lila raised her eyebrows. "What do I *think*? I think you're planning on being very naughty. Am I right?"

Jessica dimpled. "C'mon, I want to try a few of these on."

They retreated to a dressing room with armfuls of wispy silk-and-lace gowns. As Jessica modeled the first one, a flouncy powder-blue baby doll, Lila gaped at the plunging neckline and demanded, "What's up? Spill it, Wakefield!"

"Well . . ." Jessica paused to pull off the gown and slip on another, prolonging the suspense. "Last night Jeremy and I had a *very* intense conversation."

"You did? About what?"

"About *us*." Jessica twirled; the black chiffon gown swirled sensuously around her body. "About the depth of our love."

She could see that Lila was nearly exploding with curiosity. "What *about* the depth of your love?"

"Well, about how we might go about showing each other how deep it is."

"You mean, getting engaged and exchanging rings isn't enough?"

Jessica shook her head. "That's just a symbol, a gesture. I'm talking about *love*—you know, *feelings*."

"Feelings." Lila clapped a hand over her mouth. "Jess, you're not talking about . . . !"

Gripping Lila's forearms, Jessica gazed deep into her eyes. "Last night Jeremy said, and these were his *exact* words, 'I don't know if I can wait until our wedding night to show you how much I love you.' And I feel the same way about it, so tomorrow night . . ."

"Ohmigod!" Lila squealed. The two girls jumped up and down, laughing and practically bouncing off the dressing-room walls. "I can't believe you're going to do it!"

"Ssh!" Jessica giggled. "Do you want the whole mall to know?"

"I still can't believe it!" said Lila, lowering her voice. "Jess, this is a big thing."

"It's a huge thing," Jessica agreed, her eyes sparkling with excitement.

"Are you sure you're ready?"

"Of course I'm sure!"

Lila shook her head. "You'll wimp out," she predicted. "You'll buy a sexy nightie, but I bet you don't go through with the deed."

Jessica puffed up, offended. "I can't believe you're reducing my love life to the level of a common dare, Lila. When *you* become a woman," she said loftily, "you'll understand that you just *know* when the time is right."

Lila laughed. "OK, OK. You're engaged, you're a *woman*, you're on some higher plane. Forgive me, O superior one."

Jessica grinned. "That's more like it."

Lila sat down on the chair in the corner of the dressing room; Jessica removed another gown from its hanger. "I still can't believe it!" Lila burst out after a moment. "Gosh, Jess, you're going to be the first of any of us."

Dressed in a midnight-blue gown, Jessica gazed admiringly at her reflection in the mirror. "It's kind of scary," she admitted.

"Do you think Liz and Todd do it?"

Jessica snorted. "Are you kidding?"

"How about your brother and his girlfriend?"

Jessica considered. Steven and Billie had been going out for a while, and they were pretty serious. "Maybe. But they're in college. I mean, not that it's OK just because you're in college. What matters is that you're committed to each other, that you love and trust each other wholeheartedly, that you've found your one and only."

"Like you and Jeremy."

Jessica nodded emphatically. "Like me and Jeremy."

Sue Gibbons stood in the dressing room at the Unique Boutique staring at her reflection in the mirror. She was wearing the cranberry silk robe she'd picked out for her wedding night in Rio with

Jeremy. With Jeremy . . . the same man who'd apparently told Jessica Wakefield that he couldn't wait until *their* wedding night to show her how much he loved her.

In the adjacent dressing room, Sue could still hear Jessica and Lila chattering and giggling. The color drained from Sue's face; her knees weakening, she sank onto the chair. Could Jeremy really have said that to Jessica? Would he take the game he was playing with Jessica that far? *And if so,* Sue wondered, *what does that say about the depth of his feelings for* me? She thought of all the hours Jeremy had spent wining and dining Jessica, while Sue was left sitting alone at the Wakefields'. Hands clenched at her sides, Sue vowed to herself that Jessica wouldn't get the chance to wear her new negligee tomorrow night, or any night with Jeremy Randall.

Chapter 5

Elizabeth shifted restlessly on the couch and made another futile effort to concentrate on her French assignment. "Liz, sit still, would you?" said Todd from the other end of the sofa.

They'd come back to Todd's house after her newspaper meeting and his basketball practice to squeeze in an hour of homework before going out for a pizza dinner. Now Elizabeth slapped her textbook shut. "Sorry, but I just can't seem to stop thinking about Sue and Jeremy and the kidnapping."

"What about it?"

"There just have to be some clues out there that we missed."

"You mean that even Sam Diamond and the police haven't managed to uncover?"

Elizabeth tapped her chin thoughtfully with

the eraser end of her pencil. "The night Sue disappeared, the night of the Halloween party, Jeremy came over to our house pretty late," she remembered. "Jessica and I were in the kitchen—she was drowning her sorrows over that louse in a midnight snack. Jeremy arrived, told us Sue was missing, and the three of us went back to the cabin to look for her."

"But you didn't find anything."

"Nothing but Sue's broken necklace," Elizabeth agreed. "And we didn't go back to the cabin with Sam because there didn't seem to be any need to—we'd checked it out thoroughly. Or had we?"

"You mean . . ."

Elizabeth sat up on the couch, her eyes glinting. "Jeremy was the one who searched the cabin. Jessica and I just prowled around in the woods, tripping over branches and scaring ourselves. We took Jeremy's word that there was nothing to see inside. But what if he was lying?"

"Why would he lie? He wanted to find Sue as much as the rest of us, right?"

"I suppose." Elizabeth couldn't shake the feeling that it was somehow important that Jeremy had kept them away from the cabin. "Todd, I'm not going to be able to think about anything else until I satisfy my curiosity about this."

Now it was Todd's turn to toss his homework aside. "Then there's only one thing to do," he declared, jumping to his feet. "What do you say we drive up to the mountains and do a little sleuthing?"

"This is an adorable restaurant," Sue said to Jeremy as the Cypress Point Cafe maître d' escorted them to a table for two by the window.

"I wanted to take you somewhere special tonight," replied Jeremy, holding out her chair. "You deserve a treat after having to be cooped up at the cabin like that. I'm just sorry we're having dinner so late—something came up at work."

Sue sat down. When he was seated, Jeremy opened his menu, but Sue kept hers closed, her hands resting flat on top of it. "Jeremy . . ." she began.

"Hmm?"

"Jeremy, did you ever bring Jessica here?"

He glanced up at her. "This place? Nah. It's too fancy." Reaching out, he gave her hand a quick squeeze. "I was saving it for you."

He started to pull his hand away, but Sue clung to it. "Jeremy . . ."

"What?"

"I was just wondering . . ." She dropped her eyes, flushing with pain and discomfort as she recalled the intimate details of the conversation she'd overheard that afternoon in the dressing room at the Unique Boutique. "What do you and Jessica *do* when you go out on dates?"

Jeremy shrugged. "I don't know. Ordinary

things. We go to restaurants, we hang out at the beach. We've played tennis a few times, seen a couple movies. Why?"

"Oh, I just . . ." Sue bit her lip, praying that she wouldn't start crying. Tears always made Jeremy lose his temper. "I just hate thinking about the two of you . . . together."

Jeremy laughed, looking pleased. "Do I detect a note of jealousy?"

"You made her fall in love with you—she thinks you're going to marry her. You must be . . . close. I mean, she probably expects that the two of you will . . . you know." Sue's face was flaming.

"She's a lovesick teenager, and if I don't watch out, she's all over me like a tent," Jeremy admitted cheerfully. "That's why I try to keep our dates in public places. I have to kiss her, Sue, I won't pretend we don't do that. But that's as far as it goes between the two of us. She doesn't mean a thing to me."

Sue sank back in her chair, limp with relief. "Oh, Jeremy, really?"

"Oh, Sue, really," he said teasingly. Smiling, he nudged her foot under the table. "You're the only one for me—you know that. I love you madly."

Sue nodded, her eyes shining. "I love you, too, Jeremy."

Jeremy returned his attention to his menu, and Sue gazed out the window. The sun was just about to set over the Pacific, a huge orange shimmering globe. *Jessica's been throwing herself at Jeremy— of course that's how it is, he's irresistible—but he puts her off as best he can,* she thought. *This whole thing about a romantic rendezvous tomorrow night, it's just Jessica's imagination. She's living in a fantasy world.*

Yes, that's it, Sue decided firmly as she opened her own menu. *Jessica's just dreaming. Nothing momentous is going to happen between her and Jeremy tomorrow night because he's saving himself for me.*

The sun was setting behind the dark pine trees as Todd and Elizabeth pulled up the bumpy dirt road that led to the Project Nature cabin. To her relief there were no other cars parked there— they'd be able to sneak in and search the cabin undetected. "I'd forgotten how creepy and isolated it is here," Elizabeth said as she stepped out of Todd's BMW. With one hand she clutched a flashlight; with the other she pulled her denim jacket closed at her neck. "Cold, too."

"It's the higher elevation," said Todd. "I bet they get snow here sometimes."

They walked toward the cabin, their feet crunching on fallen leaves. Elizabeth shivered, recalling the last time she was there. Late Halloween night, when she, Jessica, and Jeremy had come to search for Sue, the cabin and the yard surrounding it had been glowing with the spooky faces of extinguished jack-o'-lanterns. "I don't really know what I'm looking for," Elizabeth admitted to Todd. "Maybe my imagination is just working overtime."

"Now that we're here, it can't hurt to look," he pointed out. "Did you say you know where they hide the key?"

"I think I heard Jeremy say they hide it under a rock. Here, let's look."

Crouching down, Elizabeth overturned a number of rocks on the ground next to the front door. Todd did the same; after a minute he gave a shout of triumph. "Got it!"

Brushing the dirt from her hands, Elizabeth stood. She watched Todd turn the key in the lock, her heart pounding. With a muffled click the lock gave way, and the door swung open.

The cabin, used by Project Nature as a base for hiking and camping expeditions, was dark and eerie. Fumbling on the wall, Elizabeth located a light switch. "That's better," she said as the cabin's spare furnishings sprang into relief.

"It's possible people have been here since Halloween," Todd remarked as they began to roam around the first floor of the cabin, peering under furniture and checking inside drawers and cabinets. "Any clues might be gone by now."

"True," Elizabeth conceded. Hands on her hips, she raked her eyes around the living room. Next to the cavernous, cold fireplace, a shadowy staircase led to the second floor. "C'mon, let's check upstairs."

It took only a few minutes to examine the bathroom and three small bedrooms decorated with plain pine furniture. "Everything's pretty bare," observed Todd as they finished searching the last bedroom. "Nothing in the closets, no sheets on the beds, not so much as a button off a shirt. Maybe a forensics expert could spot something, dirt from someone's shoe or a hair or something like that, but I'm stumped."

Looking around the room, Elizabeth heaved a deep sigh. "I just felt sure we'd find . . . something," she said, disappointed. "I guess we're back to square one."

As they wandered back into the hallway, Elizabeth had a flash of inspiration. "Wait a minute," she cried as Todd started to descend the stairs. She was picturing the cabin from the outside: two rows of windows, upstairs and downstairs, and then one tiny window under the eaves. "The attic!"

"What attic?" Todd looked up at the ceiling. "I don't see a latch or door or anything."

"There has to be one somewhere," declared Elizabeth, dashing back into the largest of the three bedrooms. "Look. Here it is!" Todd hurried to her side. A tarnished copper latch was embedded in one of the wood ceiling beams. "Can you reach it?" Elizabeth asked.

Todd stretched. "Not quite. Here, let me give you a leg up."

Todd hoisted Elizabeth in his arms, and she grasped the latch, pulling with all her might. A trapdoor opened with a groan, revealing a set of folded-up wooden steps.

Setting Elizabeth back on her feet, Todd yanked the staircase all the way down. "Got your flashlight?"

She nodded, her eyes wide. Todd started up the creaky, flimsy steps, Elizabeth right behind him. As the beam of her flashlight sliced upward into the murky blackness of the attic, her heart pounded with fear and anticipation. *What are we going to find?*

Sue sat on the twin bed in Steven Wakefield's room, where she'd been staying since she'd arrived in Sweet Valley a few months earlier. A fashion magazine lay open on her lap, but she wasn't reading it. Eyes closed, she relived her good-night kiss with Jeremy; he'd dropped her off early because he had some Project Nature business to work on. *What is it about him?* she wondered, a dreamy smile curving her lips. Whenever his arms went around her, all her worries faded and her body melted like butter. He made her feel safe, loved, taken care of. What could be better than to spend the rest of her life with a man like that?

The phone on the bedside table rang, jolting Sue from her reverie. She glanced quickly at the clock. Jeremy was probably back in his room by now. . . . *He'll call Jessica, since he didn't get to see her tonight,* Sue guessed. *He has to go through the motions, after all, play the devoted fiancé.*

On impulse she picked up the phone after the first ring and put it to her ear, her hand covering the mouthpiece. Jessica must have picked up the extension in her room at the exact same moment. "Hello?" Sue heard her say.

"Jessica. How's my own adorable fiancée?" Jeremy murmured.

A cold, hard fist closed around Sue's heart. She'd thought Jeremy reserved that soft, sexy voice just for her. *He's pretending,* she reminded herself. *He has to make Jessica believe he's in love with her. It's all an act.*

"Jeremy! I'm so glad you called," said Jessica. "I was just thinking about you, and about . . ." She paused. "About tomorrow night."

Jeremy chuckled softly. "Me, too," he said. "I can't think about anything else. Listen, I've found the perfect place for us. A friend of mine from Project Nature has a condo by the beach, and he's gone out of town for a couple weeks—he left me the key. Off the bedroom there's a redwood deck with a hot tub overlooking the ocean—how does that sound to you?"

"Pretty good," said Jessica, laughing breathlessly.

"I'll pick you up tomorrow night at seven. And Jessica . . ."

"Hmm?"

"I'm crazy about you."

"I'm crazy about you, too," Jessica responded, her voice brimming with love and joy.

"I'll dream about you tonight."

"I dream about you *every* night. 'Bye, Jeremy."

"'Bye, Jess."

Sue replaced the receiver gently, anguished tears streaming down her face. *He is planning to seduce Jessica. He lied to me. He looked straight into my eyes at the restaurant tonight and lied to me.*

Sue stared at the wall across from the bed, a blank, defeated expression on her face. She'd wanted so much to believe in Jeremy, to believe he had her best interests at heart. He'd become her whole life; she'd be lost without him. But apparently *he* didn't really care for her at all.

A fresh spate of tears started. *Why am I so weak, darn it, why do I still love him?* Disillusioned, confused, only one thing seemed clear to Sue. Jessica Wakefield wasn't the only one who'd been living in a fantasy world.

Reaching the top step of the attic ladder, Elizabeth swung her flashlight in a wide arc. Suddenly, out of the corner of her eye she saw a movement in the shadows; at the same instant something flew against her hair and skin. "Todd, help!" she screamed, swinging wildly at whatever it was that was attacking her.

The flashlight fell from her hand and clattered to the floor. Retrieving it quickly, Todd illuminated the far corner of the attic. "Bats," he exclaimed, disgusted.

Elizabeth shuddered, her arms folded over her head. "Ugh. Let's get out of here."

"Wait a minute." Todd aimed the beam of the flashlight in the other direction. "Look, Liz!"

Together they hurried across the attic to investigate. "A chair," said Elizabeth, bending to examine it. Something was coiled under the chair. "And some rope!"

"Someone could have been tied up here," Todd deduced.

"Check out this box." With her foot Elizabeth slid a cardboard box toward Todd. "Bottled water and some cans of food," she said excitedly. "I bet someone *was* kept up here!"

"Sue?"

"Who else?"

The two stared at each other. "But she said she was driven someplace pretty far away—she was in a car for a couple of hours."

"The kidnapper could have just driven around in circles and then brought her back here. She was blindfolded," Elizabeth pointed out.

"So if Sue was held here, what does that mean?"

"It means . . ." Elizabeth remembered Jeremy's eagerness to keep her and Jessica away from the cabin the night they searched for Sue. "Jeremy Randall could be behind all of this."

"You think Jeremy kidnapped Sue?"

"It's possible. He spent a lot of time at our house while she was missing, but the cabin's close enough that he could have made trips back and forth."

"And the ransom demands were taped," Todd said. "So he could have made the tapes and then . . ." His forehead creased in a puzzled frown. "Do you think he had an accomplice? Someone had to play the tapes over the phone."

Elizabeth nodded slowly. "He must have had an accomplice. Maybe he even hired someone else to kidnap Sue. Otherwise, wouldn't she have recognized his voice or something?"

"You'd think so."

Suddenly, Todd bent over. "What is it?" Elizabeth asked.

Straightening, he showed her what he'd retrieved from the dusty floor. "Batteries."

She cocked her head to one side. "The right size for a portable tape player, maybe?"

"Maybe."

Todd pocketed the two batteries. Leaving the rest of the stuff behind, he and Elizabeth descended the ladder back to the bedroom. "What a horrible place to be held prisoner," said Elizabeth, imagining Sue's terror as she sat blindfolded, the bats fluttering and squeaking around her, not knowing whether her captors would kill her or set her free. "Jeremy had something to do with this," she said with conviction.

"I agree," said Todd, gazing earnestly into her eyes. "But how are we going to prove it?"

Elizabeth shook her head, frustrated. "That's what I don't know."

Jessica curled up under the covers in her bed. She was still tingling all over from Jeremy's phone call. "I've found the perfect place . . . a condo by the beach . . . a hot tub . . . I'll dream about you. . . ."

And I'll dream about you, Jeremy . . . sweet, sweet dreams . . . Jessica drifted off to sleep with a smile on her face. There she was at the condo, wearing the midnight-blue silk-and-lace negligee Lila had helped her choose at the Unique Boutique. She stepped out onto the redwood deck—a cool night breeze fingered her hair and skin—and someone turned to her, a glass of champagne in each hand. . . .

Jessica held out her arms, but it wasn't Jeremy. It was Sue, and now, instead of champagne, she was holding a gun. Jessica opened her mouth to scream, "Sue, no!" but she was paralyzed, helpless, as Sue raised the gun, her finger tightening on the trigger. . . .

Jessica sat bolt upright in bed, drenched in sweat with her heart hammering. "A dream," she whispered to herself, panting with relief. "It was just a—"

At that moment a shadowy figure flitted toward the foot of her bed. Jessica opened her mouth to scream for real this time, but before she could utter a sound, the figure raised a finger to its lips. "Ssh, Jessica, it's only me, Sue."

Jessica shrank back against her pillows, clutching the blanket to her throat. Sue didn't appear to have a gun, but that didn't mean Jessica's dream wasn't coming true. *She's come to get me, to get revenge on me for stealing her fiancé!* Jessica thought, her mouth dry. "Wh-what do you want?" she squeaked.

"I just want to talk to you."

Sue switched on the light on Jessica's nightstand, then sat down on the edge of the bed. Jessica blinked in the sudden brightness. "What about?"

"About you and Jeremy," Sue said, her expression solemn.

"I don't want to hear it," Jessica replied curtly. "You're just going to try to tell me he's wrong for me, he'll let me down, I'm making a mistake. You still think you can get him back, don't you?"

Sue pressed her lips together in a tight line. "I don't need to get him back. He never left me."

Jessica stared, beginning to suspect that at long last Sue had gone over the edge. "What are you talking about?"

76

"It's a long story. Will you just hear me out?"

Jessica folded her arms across her chest. "If I do, will you leave me and Jeremy alone once and for all?"

Sue nodded. "OK, I'm listening."

Sue drew in a deep, shaky breath. "It started after my mother died," she began, twisting a corner of the blanket nervously in her hands. "Jeremy and I had recently become engaged after dating for a month, and I knew Mom disapproved of him. She came right out and told me she thought he was only after my money and said she'd disinherit me if I went through with the wedding. I didn't take her seriously, but I should have. At the last minute she altered her will so that the money would go to your mother instead."

Jessica rolled her eyes impatiently. "This is old news, Sue. Tell me something I don't already know."

"Jeremy was with me when the will was read," Sue continued. "And he . . ." She shuddered at the recollection. "I'd never seen anyone so angry. He was enraged, and I was naive enough to think he was enraged on my behalf."

Jessica tipped her head to one side, puzzled. "But he didn't care about the money. He wanted to marry you anyway, right?"

"For a couple of days I thought we'd put the whole thing behind us," said Sue, not answering the question directly. "The terms of the will were that I could get the money only if I permanently ended my relationship with Jeremy. I wasn't about to do that. I was disappointed about the money, but Jeremy was more important to me; he agreed that we'd just have to make the best of the situation. We still had each other, and that was what mattered. But then . . ."

She paused, then went on, with apparent effort. "Out of the blue he started asking all these questions about your mom, your family, about Sweet Valley. I'd visited you all with my parents when I was a little girl, but I didn't remember much about the trip. I knew our mothers had been dedicated correspondents, though, so I dug up a pile of letters Alice had written to Mom. Jeremy and I read them, one by one."

Jessica shivered involuntarily, as if ghostly fingers had touched her spine. "Why?"

"I didn't know at first myself," admitted Sue. "I thought Jeremy was just curious."

"What were the letters about?"

"Your mother wrote a lot about you and Liz," Sue told her, "about how different you were from each other, your personalities and your interests. She said she worried about *you* sometimes because you could be wild, you seemed to have a nose for trouble."

Jessica frowned. "That was an invasion of privacy—you shouldn't have read them."

"I know," said Sue sadly. "I wish we hadn't.

But we did, and from that moment Jeremy became obsessed."

"With what?" asked Jessica.

"With *you*."

Jessica was completely befuddled. "Me?"

"You were all he talked about," Sue confirmed. "He read and reread the stuff about you in the letters until he knew it by heart. At first I was jealous. I didn't understand why he was so taken with a girl he'd never met. But then I began to catch on."

"Catch on . . . ?"

"To Jeremy's scheme."

"Jeremy's scheme," Jessica repeated, her head whirling as she tried to keep pace with Sue's bizarre narrative.

"One day he said, 'The only way for your money to revert back to you is if we end our relationship, right?' I said that was true, but of course he was more important to me than my stupid inheritance. 'I'd never choose money over you,' I told him. That's when he said maybe I wouldn't *have* to choose. Maybe there was a way I could have them both. 'Write to Alice Wakefield and tell her you want to get married in California,' he said, 'and I'll take care of everything else.'"

"What did he mean, 'everything else'?" asked Jessica, staring at Sue with dread and fascination.

"This is the part you're not going to like," said Sue, biting her lip. "Jeremy and you . . . it was a setup."

"What?"

"From start to finish your entire relationship was just part of our plan to get my inheritance back."

"Wait a minute." Jessica raised a hand in protest, shaking her head. "It was an accident, us meeting that day on the beach. Jeremy hit me on the head with a Frisbee. It was love at first sight, it was—"

"A setup," repeated Sue.

The color drained from Jessica's face, and then she flushed a hot, angry red. "I don't believe you."

"It's the truth," Sue swore. "Jeremy knew who you were—he sought you out. And it worked just the way he wanted it to. You fell head over heels for him, and with the wedding canceled and Jeremy and I supposedly estranged, the money became mine again."

Jessica was dizzy with confusion. "But—but it couldn't have been a scheme. He couldn't have known I'd ruin the wedding," she protested. "He couldn't have predicted that."

Sue sighed heavily. "Jeremy may not be a very moral person, or a very kind person, but he's very smart. He figured out from reading your mother's letters that when it came to guys, you'd stop at nothing to get what you wanted."

Jessica gaped at Sue, shocked speechless. She thought back to that first encounter on the beach, the Frisbee, the kiss. She tried to comprehend that it was all an act, a cold-blooded ruse to get her to fall in love with Jeremy. Their entire relationship flashed before her eyes, from that first kiss and the other stolen kisses while Jeremy was still engaged to Sue, to the fateful day when Jeremy and Sue nearly became husband and wife, to the day Jeremy asked Jessica to marry him—the day she thought was the happiest of her life. *No,* Jessica thought, the blood pounding wildly in her ears. *It couldn't have been an act. Jeremy loves me—it's for real.*

"I don't believe you," she cried, her eyes flashing. "You're making this up—you're just trying to chase me away from Jeremy so you can steal him back!"

Sue shook her head gloomily. "I wish I were, but it's the truth, Jessica. And it gets . . . it gets worse."

How could it get worse? Jessica wondered, dazed.

"When you and Jeremy were engaged—when he said he was in Costa Rica—he was still here. He and I were still seeing each other."

"But I called him in Costa Rica!" exclaimed Jessica.

"You dialed a number in Costa Rica, but someone else always answered the phone and took a message, right?" said Sue. "That was a friend of Jeremy's—he'd pass the message on, and Jeremy would call you back. Jeremy was in California the whole time."

Jessica remembered the video-club film about the most romantic places to kiss in Sweet Valley, and her momentary impression that she'd glimpsed Jeremy and Sue in the background of one of the shots. "No," she whispered.

Sue dropped the final bombshell. "The kidnapping was a hoax, too," she concluded, "a last-resort way to get the money because we thought you and Liz were going to blow our cover. But you didn't, so it turned out to be unnecessary."

Jessica recalled her horrible suspicion on Tuesday night when she studied the videotape of the ransom drop-off. Despite the evidence, she'd repressed her suspicions about Jeremy then, and now she repressed them again. "If—and I say *if*— any of this is true, why would you tell me?"

"Because I realize I've made a terrible mistake," said Sue. "I may not come across so well in all this, Jessica, but Jeremy . . . he's a bad person. He's just consumed by his desire for money—he doesn't know when to stop. I started to realize that when he came up with the kidnapping ploy. I saw what serious trouble we were getting ourselves into, and I tried to talk him out of it. I was ready to call the whole thing off, but he wouldn't listen to me. He didn't care about me anymore—it was just the money. I think . . ." Sue's voice cracked; tears glistened in her eyes. "I think my mother was right about him."

Jessica looked at Sue with mistrust. "I still don't

understand why you would tell me this."

"Because I know about your big plans for tomorrow night," Sue said, rising to her feet. "Do yourself a favor, Jessica. Don't go. I've told you this so you can protect yourself. Jeremy's only using you, just like he's been using me. He isn't going to marry you."

She knows about my plans for tomorrow night? But how . . . ? "You've been spying on us!" Jessica cried. "You've been spying on us and eavesdropping, and you're just jealous! That's why you've told me all these horrible lies!"

"Oh, Jessica." Sue sighed tiredly. "I didn't have to eavesdrop. I didn't have to spy. Jeremy's been telling me everything. Well, almost everything."

And then Sue repeated, word for word, one of Jessica and Jeremy's most intimate conversations. In the same emotionless monotone Sue related details of a date Jessica had gone on with Jeremy— little personal details she never could have known unless Jeremy or Jessica had told her about them. *And I certainly didn't tell her,* Jessica thought, her face white as paper. That could mean only one thing. . . .

"Get out," Jessica whispered hoarsely.

Instead of turning to leave, Sue stretched out a hand, her face filled with sorrow and compassion. "Now you know the truth about him and about me, and you can do whatever you want with it. I'm not going to tell him that you know—I think it's safer for you that way. I suppose you could turn us in, but I hope you'll—"

Jessica raised her voice. "I said get out!"

Silently, Sue slipped from the room. Flinging herself down onto the bed, Jessica buried her face in the pillow and burst into tears.

Chapter 6

Friday morning Jessica sat on the edge of her bed, staring at the phone on her nightstand. Pick it up, she commanded herself. But when she reached out, her hand was shaking; her entire body trembled uncontrollably. She couldn't do it.

"It can't be true," Jessica whispered, her throat constricting with tears. "It must have been a dream—a terrible dream." But she could still see Sue sitting on the edge of her bed, and every word Sue had spoken was imprinted on Jessica's brain in letters of fire. It wasn't a dream; it was cold, hard, cruel reality.

Jessica still hadn't fully absorbed the depth of Sue and Jeremy's deception, the perverse complexity of their nefarious scheme, but she'd grasped one thing all too well. *Jeremy lied to me from the very first moment we met. He's been toying with me, leading me on. He pretended to care, to be committed, even tried to get me in bed, while all along he was planning to desert me and run off with Sue.*

She remembered her tumultuous emotions of just a few nights ago when she thought she recognized the kidnapper in the videotape. Out of love for Jeremy she'd convinced herself she was mistaken, when the whole time both Jeremy *and* Sue were guilty . . . guilty as sin. . . .

There was an open box sticking out from under her bed. Bending down, Jessica lifted the lid. Inside, the midnight-blue silk nightgown nestled in a bed of tissue paper. Replacing the lid, Jessica shoved the box deep under her bed. Then, her face deathly white, she picked up the telephone. She dialed Jeremy's number fast, before she could lose her nerve.

"Yeah? Who is it?" he mumbled into the phone.

Just twelve hours earlier Jeremy's sleepy, sexy voice would have thrilled Jessica to her core. Now she had to fight back a wave of nausea. "Jeremy, it's me, Jessica," she said weakly.

"Is something wrong? You sound terrible."

"I'm sick," she lied. "I think I have a bad case of the flu. I can't—I'm not going to be able to make it tonight, you know, the date at your friend's condo. I guess . . . I'll have to give you a rain check. I hope that's . . . I hope you're not mad."

"Aw, Jess." Jeremy chuckled. "Don't worry

about it. You're worth waiting for. I just hope you perk up. Feel better, OK?"

"OK," she whispered.

"I love you, Jess. Talk to you soon."

"'Bye."

As Jessica hung up the phone, her stomach lurched violently. She raced into the bathroom and knelt by the toilet. She didn't get sick, though. Slowly, the feeling of revulsion subsided, leaving her weary, desolate, empty. Pressing her face against the cool porcelain, Jessica closed her eyes and wept.

"Don't take this the wrong way, but you look like death warmed over," Elizabeth said when Jessica entered the kitchen for breakfast.

Jessica watched her sister slice a ripe, juicy cantaloupe into wedges, the nausea rising again. "I . . . I didn't sleep that well. I think I'm coming down with something," she mumbled.

"Maybe you should stay home from school today," Elizabeth suggested.

Jessica shrugged. She'd considered it, but she had a hunch it would only make her feel worse to lie around the house all day brooding about Jeremy's betrayal. "I'll be all right."

"How about a piece of toast or something?"

"Actually, I think I'll just . . ." Suddenly Jessica knew she had to get out of the house or risk breaking down in front of Elizabeth. "Do you think you could call Todd or Enid, hitch a ride with one of them? I want to get to school early. There are a couple of things I need to take care of."

"Sure." Elizabeth shot a puzzled look her way. "Are you sure you're OK? Maybe you should—"

Jessica didn't hear the rest of Elizabeth's sentence; she was already stepping into the garage and closing the door behind her.

I can't tell Liz, Jessica thought as she steered the Jeep toward Sweet Valley High. *I can't tell anyone.* Maybe Sue and Jeremy were breaking every law in the book, but it would be too mortifying to admit to the world how completely she'd been fooled. She didn't care if they got away with the money that should have been Mrs. Wakefield's. Jessica just wanted Sue Gibbons and Jeremy Randall out of her life.

When Jessica arrived, the halls of the high school were deserted; homeroom wouldn't start for forty minutes. Opening her locker, Jessica dumped her books inside, then slammed the door shut again. She leaned back against the locker, staring dully down the long, empty corridor.

She was still standing there half an hour later as the halls began to fill with bustling, chattering students. Jessica entered the crowd, waving and exchanging greetings with her friends. Inside, though, she felt as if she were still standing by the locker, watching everything from a distance. She'd come to school hoping to get her mind off what

Sue and Jeremy had done to her, but of course that was impossible. How could she think about anything else?

I can't believe Sue wormed her way into our family under false pretenses, like a poisonous snake, Jessica raged silently as she made her way to homeroom. *And we all felt so sorry for her, we went to so much trouble, especially Mom and Dad. The wedding, and when she took all those pills, and when we thought she was kidnapped . . . and it was all a scam!*

As for Jeremy . . . Conflicting emotions battled in Jessica's heart. On the one hand, she hated Sue for destroying her love for Jeremy by telling her the truth about him, but on the other . . . Walking down the hall, Jessica hugged her notebook tight against her chest. For so many weeks she'd felt detached from life at Sweet Valley High; all she thought about was Jeremy and the life they were embarking on together. Now suddenly she wanted nothing more than to blend into the crowd and disappear. Yes, she was hurt, angry, and disgusted, but also grateful. In the nick of time Sue had talked Jessica out of sacrificing her virginity to Jeremy. *Or to anyone, for that matter,* Jessica realized. If she'd given herself to Jeremy, she would have lost irrevocably something she just wasn't ready to give up—physically *or* emotionally. There was a lot she didn't understand about this triangle she'd become entangled in, but one thing was suddenly glaringly clear. She was way too young . . . for any of this.

The final bell rang, and Jessica joined the flood of students hurrying to their lockers in a rush to escape into the warm afternoon sunshine. *This has been the longest day of my life,* Jessica thought morosely as she dialed the combination of her locker. *And tonight will probably be the longest night of my life.* How was she going to get her mind off Jeremy . . . and what she had come so dangerously close to doing with him?

"Hi, Jess, I'm glad I caught you."

Jessica glanced up to see Ken, looking cute in faded jeans and a weathered denim shirt. "Hi, yourself," she said with a halfhearted smile.

"I couldn't help overhearing at lunch how . . . I mean, not that I was listening in or anything." He grinned, flushing slightly. "But when you were talking with Lila, and you said your plans for tonight had changed . . ."

Jessica's cheeks turned pink. How much had Ken overheard?

"I just thought maybe now you'd be able to make it to the Dairi Burger after the game," he explained. "What do you say?"

"I'm just not . . ." Jessica caught herself. *In the mood,* she'd been about to say. Then she remembered Ken's sweet words the previous day. "We haven't seen much of you lately. We miss you. . . ."

He was waiting for her answer, a hopeful smile on his handsome face. Jessica looked up, straight into his eyes. Honest, friendly eyes, not like Jeremy's. . . . "I'd love to go out with you guys tonight," she said in a clear, sure voice.

"The art-supply store?" Jessica said fifteen minutes later as Lila parked the Triumph in front of Paints Plus in downtown Sweet Valley. "Hey, I thought we were going to the mall. What are we doing here?"

Lila stalked purposefully into the store, Jessica trotting at her heels. "Buying art supplies, what do you think?" She marched over to a display of oil paints in white tubes. "OK, let's go to it. I think we're going to need one of each color."

Lila started loading Jessica's arms with tubes of paint. "Paintbrushes," Lila muttered, grabbing a bunch of various sizes off the racks, "and a palette and paint thinner and, of course, an easel . . ."

Ten minutes later they were back in the car. Jessica had a heavy paper bag on her lap; six pre-stretched canvases and a collapsible wooden easel were sticking out of the Triumph's tiny trunk. "OK, Li, start talking," Jessica commanded. "What on earth are you up to?"

Starting the engine, Lila flashed Jessica a brilliant, self-satisfied smile. "Since Robby doesn't seem to be getting anywhere with his paintings for the gallery exhibit, *I'm* going to paint them for him."

91

Jessica gaped at her. "You're going to paint them for him? What do *you* know about painting?"

"You smear some paint on the canvas and call it modern art," Lila said with a careless wave. "How hard could it be?"

"If it wasn't hard, we'd all be Rembrandts and Monets!"

"I didn't *say* I think I can paint like *Rembrandt*," Lila pointed out as she turned into the driveway of Fowler Crest. "I'm going to try an abstract style."

Jessica helped Lila lug the canvases and easel into one of the guest bedrooms on the second floor of the spacious, elegant mansion. "Are you sure you want to do this in the house?" she asked doubtfully.

Lila returned from the linen closet with an armful of snow-white sheets, which she proceeded to spread all over the floor. "Why not?"

"What if you get paint on the bedspread or something?"

Lila looked at her friend impatiently. "Jess, I think my artwork is slightly more important than a few bed linens."

When the easel was set up with a blank canvas resting on it, Lila turned to Jessica. "OK, how do you want to pose?"

"Me? You're going to paint *me*?"

"It's you or a bowl of fruit," Lila said testily. "How about posing nude? Real artists always paint nudes."

Jessica snorted. "You've got to be kidding."

"Well, then just sit on the bed. That's right, lean back on one arm and kind of throw your hair over one shoulder. That's good—very arty looking. OK, now, don't budge—don't even *breathe!*"

Lila squeezed bright blobs of oil paint onto her palette and selected a medium-size brush. Blending some red and yellow, she dabbed tentatively at the canvas. "Hey, this is fun," she said a short while later. Her brush strokes were getting bigger and bolder; she'd already covered nearly half the canvas with paint.

Jessica yawned. "For you, maybe. My arm is falling asleep—I can feel the pins and needles starting." She rolled her shoulder slightly.

"I said, don't budge!"

The portrait was completed to Lila's satisfaction in less than an hour. "So, do you want to see it?" she asked Jessica.

Jessica jumped up, stretching her arms over her head. "I am so stiff," she groaned, crossing the room to Lila's side. "This had better be . . ."

When she saw the portrait, Jessica's eyes widened. "Well, what do you think?" Lila prompted eagerly.

To Lila's annoyance Jessica burst out laughing. "Ohmigod, it's horrible!" Jessica exclaimed. "It's the worst painting I've ever seen! My face is *blue!*"

"It's abstract, modern," Lila said defensively. "I was painting your *mood,* not your skin tone."

"And look at my legs. They look like dying snakes!"

"Well, you kept uncrossing and recrossing them—you were wiggling like a snake. Oh, what do you know about art, anyway!"

"I don't know much, but I know this stinks," Jessica said, wrinkling her nose. "Are you really going to hang this on the wall at the gallery and pretend Robby painted it?"

Lila nodded. "It doesn't stink. And even if it did, it would still be better than nothing."

Jessica looked at the painting again and grimaced. "Don't be so sure!"

"Go, Gladiators!" Jessica screamed, jumping up and down on the sidelines of the football field with the rest of the Sweet Valley High cheerleading squad. "C'mon. Go, Ken. Go, Scott!"

There was less than a minute left on the clock in the fourth quarter; it was third and ten for the Sweet Valley team, which was down by four points. Ken had the ball on Big Mesa's twenty-yard line; it was all up to him.

"If he tries that pass to Scottie again, he'll just get sacked," Maria predicted, chewing her fingernails.

The clock was still running; Jessica held her breath. She heard Ken call the play, and then he was dancing backward, setting up the pass to Scott Trost, the wide receiver. Jessica winced as the Big Mesa defense converged on Scottie. "Oh, no . . . !"

Suddenly the entire home-team bleachers erupted in a roar. Instead of passing to Scottie, Ken had feinted to the left and handed the ball off to running back Bryce Fisherman. Miraculously dodging his burly opponents, Bryce ran the ball into Big Mesa's end zone. "Touchdown!" Jessica shouted, grabbing Maria and whirling her in a dizzy victory circle.

It was a jubilant group that crowded into the Dairi Burger after the game. Jessica had gotten a ride with Ken, who was so busy high-fiving everyone he met that it took about twenty minutes for him to make his way to the rear of the restaurant.

Elizabeth, Todd, Bruce, Pamela, Amy, Barry, Maria, Winston, Bill, and DeeDee were already settled into a couple of big booths, chatting over menus that they didn't even need to look at because they knew the Dairi Burger's offerings by heart.

"Great game, Matthews," boomed Bruce.

"Thanks, Patman." Ken, his blond hair still wet from a postgame shower, squeezed in next to Pamela while Jessica sat down opposite him next to Maria. "It was too close for comfort, though, let me tell ya."

"But you pulled it off. Hey, Jess." Jessica felt Winston kick her lightly under the table. "Good to see you."

Jessica smiled. "Good to be here."

"Where's Jeremy?" asked Pamela.

"Oh, he . . ." Jessica felt Ken's eyes on her face and blushed. "He's got things to do for Project Nature this weekend."

"I suppose he's not into high-school stuff like football games anyway," commented Maria.

"No," agreed Jessica, shifting uncomfortably on her seat. "Not really."

"So how're the plans for the Mistletoe Madness dance coming along?" Winston asked cochairs Bruce and Pamela.

"It's gonna be great," Bruce predicted with his usual arrogance. "The best dance ever."

"I like the mistletoe theme, anyway," Winston said, pursing his lips and aiming a smack in Maria's direction.

She laughed. "Any excuse, right?"

"What's your story, Matthews?" asked Bruce. "The dance, I mean. Are you going to fly solo?"

Ken and his longtime girlfriend, Terri Adams, had broken up recently, making Ken one of Sweet Valley High's most eligible bachelors. "There must be some girl out there who'd take you on as a charity case," Winston joked.

"I was thinking of taking out a personal ad, actually," Ken quipped back.

The evening flew by; too soon Ken was dropping off Jessica at her house on Calico Drive. "Sounds like people might be going to the Beach Disco tomorrow night," he called after her as she hopped out of the car. "I mean, if Jeremy's not around—if you're looking for something to do . . ."

"Maybe," Jessica replied, waving. "Or I'll see you in school on Monday. Thanks for the ride."

"Anytime."

Jessica watched Ken drive away, a smile still lingering on her lips. They hadn't done anything out of the ordinary—just burgers, fries, and shakes at the Dairi Burger—but for some reason the evening felt incredibly special to her. *It was just like old times*, she realized with a pang. *I felt like a high-school kid again, for the first time since . . .*

Since Jeremy. Gulping, Jessica turned to trudge up the walk. For a few magical hours she'd laughed and joked with her friends and forgotten all about the insanity of the rest of her life. *I'll deal with it tomorrow*, she told herself tiredly. Tomorrow she'd think of a way to break up with Jeremy so that he didn't suspect anything. Then she'd just have to sit tight and wait for him and Sue to get out of Sweet Valley. *Then I'll have my life back again.*

"I think I should go inside," Elizabeth whispered to Todd, disentangling herself from his embrace.

It was past midnight, and they were parked by the curb in front of her house. Todd released her with a reluctant sigh. "It's just that I could kiss you all night," he murmured, stroking her hair back from her forehead. "You're just the most huggable girl I know."

Elizabeth smiled. "I'd better be the *only* huggable girl you know!"

Their lips met in one last, sweet, lingering kiss. "See you tomorrow," Elizabeth promised.

"I love you," said Todd.

She waved good-bye as he drove off, then hurried toward the house. She could see a light on in Jessica's window; Sue's bedroom, meanwhile, was dark. Inside, Elizabeth tiptoed upstairs, then knocked softly on her sister's door. "Jess?" she whispered. "Can I come in?"

She heard a soft murmur and pushed open the door. Wearing the oversize football jersey she slept in, Jessica was sitting on the edge of her bed brushing out her hair. "I just wanted to say good night," Elizabeth said. "It was a nice surprise that you showed up at the Dairi Burger. I didn't expect—I mean, I figured you'd be going out with Jeremy." Elizabeth bit her tongue to keep from asking if this meant that Jessica was getting ready to cool things off with Jeremy. "It almost felt like old times, that's all," she finished, smiling shyly.

To Elizabeth's surprise Jessica's face crumpled. "Oh, Liz," Jessica cried, pressing her hands to her eyes and bursting into tears.

"Jess, what's wrong?" Elizabeth strode to the bed and sat down next to Jessica, putting an arm around her shoulders.

"I—I can't tell you," Jessica sobbed brokenly. "You'd only say you told me so, you knew it all along, and even though you're right, I don't want to hear it. Liz, I've been such a fool!"

Jessica cried even harder. Elizabeth patted her back. "Just take a deep breath and tell me about it," she encouraged. "I promise I won't say I told you so, no matter what it is."

Jessica wiped her nose on the sleeve of her jersey, sniffling. "You won't believe it, you simply won't believe it. I almost didn't believe it myself."

"Well, try me," said Elizabeth.

By the time Jessica finished recounting everything Sue had told her the night before, Elizabeth's eyes were big and round. "I can't believe it!" she exclaimed, shocked.

"See? Isn't it the most insane, outrageous story you've ever heard?"

"I can't believe anyone could be so mercenary, and so cruel!" Elizabeth's eyes flashed. "I haven't had a good feeling about this guy, Jess, I won't pretend otherwise, but I never would have guessed he was *that* rotten."

"Tell me about it," Jessica said grimly. "I feel like the stupidest, most naive person ever born, falling for all that fake charm. I thought I wanted to *marry* him. I thought I wanted to—" She buried her face in her hands again, her shoulders shaking with suppressed sobs.

Elizabeth hugged Jessica close. "What a slime," she said, outraged on her sister's behalf. "And Sue! Faking her own kidnapping!" She shook her head

99

in disbelief. "From the very beginning we've treated her like one of the family, and the whole time . . . Well, this sure explains all her weird behavior. And it explains what Todd and I found last night at the Project Nature cabin."

Elizabeth told Jessica about how she and Todd drove out to the cabin to do some sleuthing and what they discovered in the attic. "They were in on it together," Jessica confirmed. "Sue didn't say anything about being tied up, but they probably made it look that way so if anyone found her, they wouldn't realize it was a hoax. She played the ransom demand herself over the phone."

Elizabeth shivered. "It's so cold and calculating. Jeremy and Sue have been using all of us, Jess, not just you. When I think about how worried we've all been about Sue . . . !"

For a minute the two sisters sat in silence, pondering. Then Jessica looked at Elizabeth, her eyes red-rimmed. "So what do we do now?"

Elizabeth thought about Sam Diamond and the police, on the trail of a kidnapper who'd been right under their noses the whole time. "Maybe Sue thinks we'll keep quiet out of loyalty, but I don't think we owe her anything," she declared, her eyes flashing with righteous indignation. "I say we go to the authorities first thing in the morning."

Chapter 7

At nine A.M. on Saturday morning, Jessica sat on her sister's bed watching Elizabeth dial Sam Diamond's phone number in Los Angeles. "Shoot, she's not in the office on weekends—it's just her voice mail," exclaimed Elizabeth, hanging up the phone.

"Why didn't you leave a message?"

"I didn't know what to say." Quickly, Elizabeth punched in the phone number for L.A. information. "I'd like the number for Samantha Diamond, please," she requested. A few seconds later she shook her head. "No, not her business number—do you have a home number? Thanks anyway."

"She's unlisted," said Jessica. "Well, we could always ask Dad for her home number—I bet he has it."

Elizabeth sank back in her desk chair, a frown wrinkling her forehead. "We could," she admitted, "but then we'd have to tell him why we want it."

Jessica nodded slowly. "I see what you mean."

"I'm just not ready to do that," said Elizabeth. "Gosh, when Mom and Dad find out what Sue's been up to . . . !"

"They'll feel so betrayed," Jessica anticipated. "They might not even believe it. I mean, let's face it—they're pretty sympathetic to Sue, and I've been in the doghouse lately. They'd probably think I made it all up to smear Sue."

"I still don't know what to think myself," said Elizabeth, twisting a strand of her silky blond hair. "I mean, I *like* Sue. We were friends—at least I *thought* we were. I just don't understand how she could get involved in something like this—and with someone like Jeremy. If Jeremy's as bad as she says, that is. I mean, she's not stupid—she's a smart girl. Why would she go along with him? Is she a bad person, is she just lonely, or boy crazy, or spineless and impressionable, or what?"

Boy crazy, spineless, impressionable . . . sounds a lot like me, Jessica thought, making a wry face. "I guess she's just greedy. She wants to get that money back."

"I was so mad at her when you told me about this last night," related Elizabeth, "but now . . ." She sighed heavily. "The fact that Sue came to you shows she's not totally selfish. It shows that she's started to realize she's making a huge mistake. I feel sorry for her in a way. She's backed herself into a corner with Jeremy—clearly she's unhappy."

"So what do you think we should do?" Jessica asked somewhat impatiently. She personally thought it was a waste of time and energy to feel sorry for Sue. "Wait until Monday and call Sam again?"

"I don't think we can afford to wait," said Elizabeth grimly. "If it were just Sue . . . She's trapped—she can't make a move until she's sure the money is hers. But I think Jeremy Randall is a dangerous person. We'll have to go to the police with the story Sue told you."

"They'll never believe it," predicted Jessica.

"We'll bring the videotape," proposed Elizabeth, "and you can tell them that you're ready to identify the kidnapper. Supposedly the inquiry has stalled for lack of leads . . . well, wait until they get a load of this!"

Elizabeth and Jessica marched up to the reception desk at the Sweet Valley police station, videotape in hand. "We'd like to speak with either Detective Carlisle or Detective Belsky, if they're in, please," said Elizabeth, naming the two officers who'd interviewed Sue and the Wakefield family on Tuesday night.

"Do you have an appointment?"

"No, but we have some important evidence about the Sue Gibbons kidnapping case," Elizabeth announced.

The receptionist raised her eyebrows. •Picking up a phone, she spoke briefly with someone, then nodded to the twins. "Detective Belsky can see you—she's down the hall, third door on the right."

"I don't think I can do this," Jessica whispered nervously to Elizabeth as they approached the detective's office. "I can't tell that story—it's so awful, and it makes me look like such an idiot."

Elizabeth squeezed her sister's hand. "Don't blame yourself," she said, soothing but stern. "You're not the bad guy, Jeremy is. And we're going to nail him."

They knocked on the door. "Come in," Detective Belsky called out.

Looking up from her computer screen, the detective waved the twins into two chairs facing her desk. "I'm very curious," she declared. "You have evidence relating to the kidnapping case?"

Elizabeth looked at Jessica, who drew a long, shaky breath. "It's kind of a bizarre story," Jessica began weakly. "I'll try to give it to you exactly as Sue Gibbons gave it to me. . . ."

True to her promise, Jessica presented the whole sordid, outrageous story, not leaving out a single detail or plot twist. Elizabeth knew it pained her sister to confess how badly she'd been taken in by Jeremy Randall, but Jessica forged ahead bravely, stopping only once to sniffle discreetly and then recompose herself.

By the time Jessica was finished with her narrative, Detective Belsky's mouth was hanging open. Snapping it shut, she narrowed her eyes at Jessica. "You're saying the whole thing was a hoax? Well, this is quite an accusation, and I'm intrigued," she remarked, drumming her fingers on the desk. "But this is hearsay. You said you had *evidence*."

"The proof is right here." Elizabeth proffered the videotape triumphantly. "Jessica filmed the kidnapper picking up the briefcase of money, and later she realized she could identify him as Jeremy Randall by the ring on his left pinkie finger."

"The ring I gave him myself," Jessica added.

"Let's see the tape," requested Detective Belsky.

Swiveling in her chair, she popped the tape into a combination TV/VCR on the table behind her. Elizabeth held her breath, her skin crawling. It would be the first time she viewed the tape knowing that the heavily disguised "kidnapper" was in fact Jeremy Randall. . . .

There was some static, and then a picture flashed onto the screen. Only it wasn't a picture of a man in a trench coat entering the phone booth near Glen's Grove gas station; instead it was the opening credits of a popular television sitcom.

Detective Belsky frowned. Elizabeth and Jessica gaped at each other. "What's this?" the detective snapped.

"Fast-forward it," begged Jessica. "I know it's there. I watched it over and over and . . ."

"Steven was home the other night, and this is his favorite show," Elizabeth moaned, remembering her brother's visit. "He taped over the kidnapper!"

Ejecting the tape, Detective Belsky tossed it across the desk and rose to her feet. "I have work to do," she said, her expression cold and severe, "so if you'd please . . ." She gestured toward the door.

"But we're telling the truth!" Elizabeth cried. "There's more proof at the Project Nature cabin. You've got to believe—"

"It's a very serious thing to falsely accuse someone of a crime," Detective Belsky interrupted. "And it's a very serious thing to waste the time of an officer of the law. Don't let me hear of you taking this prank any further."

Elizabeth and Jessica had no choice but to skulk from the office with the troublemaking videotape. Detective Belsky slammed the door behind them.

"I told you they wouldn't believe us," Jessica said to Elizabeth as they got back into the Jeep.

They'd stopped at home and then realized it wasn't the best place to talk strategy—Sue or their parents might overhear them. Elizabeth, who was driving, headed for the Dairi Burger. "She might have believed us if the stupid video hadn't been taped over," Elizabeth exclaimed. "Boy, when I get my hands on Steven . . . !"

"I bet even the videotape wouldn't have

106

helped," speculated Jessica. "Detective Belsky probably would have said what I said to myself when I first saw it—sure, the kidnapper's wearing a gold ring on the pinkie of his left hand, but lots of men wear rings. That's not enough to go by."

"So the police aren't going to help us, and we can't reach Sam." Elizabeth tightened her grip on the steering wheel, her expression determined. "That just means we'll have to bring Jeremy to justice by ourselves."

"But how are we going to do that?" wondered Jessica as they crossed the Dairi Burger parking lot a minute later.

Elizabeth shook her head. "Good question."

Inside the restaurant they chose one of the booths in the back, where they were less likely to be spotted. As they sat down, Elizabeth noticed that Jessica's cheeks were turning crimson. She turned to see what—or who—was getting her twin all hot and bothered.

Ken was standing at the counter, paying for a take-out order. Elizabeth's eyes widened. "Since when does Ken Matthews make you blush?" she demanded. "Don't tell me something happened between you two last night!"

"Relax, nothing happened," Jessica swore, her face still flaming. "Can we just get down to business here?"

"OK." Elizabeth leaned back in the booth and folded her arms. "We need a plan. We need to gather more hard evidence against Jeremy so when we go to the police again, they'll listen to us."

"Evidence against Jeremy . . . *and* against Sue," added Jessica.

Elizabeth bit her lip. "I wish . . . I wish we could do this without hurting Sue," she said.

"Sue and Jeremy are in it together," Jessica reminded her. "Don't get sentimental about her—she's *not* innocent."

"I know, but . . ." Elizabeth sighed. She couldn't quite find the words for her gut feeling that while Sue had made some serious mistakes, she wasn't an evil person at heart. "OK, I won't be sentimental. I guess our first step has got to be getting evidence that Jeremy and Sue are still seeing each other. That would prove their breakup was faked so they could get Sue's inheritance back by false pretenses."

"First of all," said Jessica, "I don't think you should let on to Sue that you know about all this. Treat her like you always do. Otherwise we might scare her and Jeremy into leaving town before we can pin anything on them."

"We need to buy ourselves some time," Elizabeth agreed. "And speaking of time, we need to find out what Sue does with hers—where she goes, if she really does meet Jeremy on the sly."

Jessica's face, which had been rosy a moment before, was now pale, and her stomach felt queasy. She forced herself to be cold and clinical about the matter. "Maybe we could borrow Amy's camcorder again. If we could catch Jeremy and Sue together on tape . . ."

"And make sure no one records over *this* tape!" Elizabeth nodded. "I think that's the route we should take. We'll catch Sue and Jeremy in a compromising position, and then . . ." Jessica had closed her eyes; her face was pained and tense. "I know it's hard to talk like this, Jess," Elizabeth said softly. "I think you're really brave to face this stuff about Jeremy head-on."

"I don't *feel* brave," Jessica said tiredly. "I feel crummy."

"Look, I'll do the dirty work," Elizabeth volunteered. "Maybe it'll be easier if you don't have to actually rub your nose in it, you know?"

"No." Jessica shook her head. "No, I think I should be the one to go after them." She knew there was still a tiny, foolish part of her heart that hoped it was all some sick, crazy lie on Sue's part. Her love for Jeremy had been too strong to be killed outright; there were still some stubborn feelings that refused to let go. "The sooner I face up to the truth," she said, her eyes hard and dry, "the better."

The phone was ringing when Jessica and Elizabeth entered the house half an hour later. Jessica picked it up in the kitchen, expecting it to be Lila again. "Hello?"

"Jess? It's me. How are you feeling? You sound a lot better than you did yesterday."

At the sound of Jeremy's voice, Jessica's stomach tightened in a knot. It wasn't hard to pretend she still felt sick. "Actually, I'm still in bed," she said, praying Jeremy hadn't spotted her and Elizabeth zooming around Sweet Valley in the Jeep that morning.

"Wish I could be there with you," Jeremy said with a meaningful chuckle.

Jessica blanched, suddenly recalling that if things had gone as originally planned, she would have already slept with Jeremy. *I would've regretted that for the rest of my life. . . .* "It's probably safer to stay away," she finally managed to choke out. "I'm pretty sure I'm contagious."

"I could at least bring over some chicken soup," he offered.

"No, you don't have to—it's better if you . . ." *Stop stuttering,* Jessica commanded herself, drawing in a deep breath. *Be cool. Don't give the game away.* "Thanks, you're incredibly sweet, but I'd really feel bad if I made you sick, too. I'll call you when I'm up and around again, OK?"

"OK. Do you still love me, Jess?"

You have to say it. You have to keep up the charade. He can't know you're onto him. "Of course I still love you, Jeremy—more than anything."

"I can't wait for us to be together, just the two of us, like we talked about the other night."

"Me, either," she whispered. "See ya."

As she hung up the phone, on the verge of gagging, Jessica glimpsed a motion in the hall beyond the kitchen. Stepping to the doorway, she looked out in time to see Sue flitting up the stairs to the second floor. *Was she eavesdropping?* Jessica wondered.

Well, two could play that game. Jessica tiptoed up the stairs and down the carpeted hallway. Sue had retreated into Steven's bedroom, closing the door behind her. Pushing the hair behind her ear, Jessica shamelessly pressed the side of her face against the door and strained to hear.

Her hunch had been right. After listening to Jessica on the phone with Jeremy, Sue had run upstairs to call Jeremy herself. "I don't know what's up with Jessica," Jessica heard Sue saying. "If she says she's sick, she's probably sick." There was a long pause; Jessica held her breath. "That sounds good to me," Sue said at last. "Can I see you before then, though? How about tonight since Jessica's out of the picture for a while?"

Tonight, Jessica thought, her heart pounding. *I'm going to catch them together tonight!*

"Eight thirty by the fountain at Hampshire Place," Sue said, referring to a new mall in Sunset Hills, a nearby town. "Yeah, that should be safe— everyone around here goes to the Valley Mall. Great, I'll see you then."

Jessica dashed down the hall to her room,

closing the door noiselessly behind her. Her heart was pounding, both from the danger of eavesdropping and in anticipation of the night that lay ahead.

Because when Jeremy and Sue met by the fountain at Hampshire Place, Jessica planned to be hidden nearby filming the whole scene.

Chapter 8

Sue drove toward Hampshire Place, humming to a song on the car radio. She wasn't in a happy mood, but she felt better than she had in days. Apparently, her warning to Jessica had had the intended impact—Jessica seemed to be pulling back from Jeremy. At the same time, as far as Sue could tell, Jessica hadn't told anyone else about their conversation. *Elizabeth's treating me just the same as always,* Sue thought, *and so are Alice and Ned. Maybe in order to protect herself, Jessica's going to protect me and Jeremy, too. Maybe we're in the clear—maybe we're going to pull this thing off after all.*

The thought should have filled her with elation, but for some reason Sue found her eyes suddenly brimming with tears. Maybe she and Jeremy *were* in the clear; maybe they'd succeed in their scheme to regain her inheritance and run off together to

Rio. *But what about love?* Sue wondered. *What about trust?* Could any amount of money make up for the fact that Jeremy had turned out to be very different from the man she'd fallen in love with, that he was willing to lie, cheat, and worse in order to get what he wanted? *And someday, if another woman comes along with more money than me, how long will he stick around?*

Reaching down, she turned up the volume on the radio, determined to drown out these depressing thoughts. She'd committed herself to Jeremy and to his greedy, dangerous schemes—she had no one else to turn to, nowhere else to go. The words of the wedding vows they hadn't yet exchanged echoed in Sue's brain. For richer or poorer, for better or worse . . .

Wearing dark sunglasses and with her hair tucked up under an L.A. Dodgers baseball cap, Jessica paced up and down in front of the shops at Hampshire Place, repeatedly glancing at the wristwatch she'd borrowed from Elizabeth. Quarter past eight, twenty minutes past, twenty-five . . .

Three minutes short of eight thirty, Jessica strolled nonchalantly to the mall's central courtyard and fountain. Under a skylight a thick cluster of palms and flowering shrubs created the perfect cover. Trying not to draw attention to herself, she huddled on the stone bench nearest the palms, Amy's camcorder ready on her lap.

Maybe they won't show, she thought, her hands shaking so much it took three tries before she was able to snap off the lens cap. *Maybe they'll decide it's too risky.* Jessica recognized that she was starting to hope Jeremy and Sue *wouldn't* show. She just wasn't sure she was ready to see Sue's story confirmed, to see the man who was supposed to be her fiancé, the man she'd been wildly in love with, rushing into the arms of his ex.

A new angle occurred to Jessica as the clock continued to tick. *Maybe this is too risky for me.* She chewed her lip nervously. *What if Jeremy sees me? What would he do? What would I say?*

Just as she was about to scramble for the exit and wait for another opportunity to tail Sue, Jeremy appeared on the other side of the courtyard. Jessica sank back down on the bench, hunching her shoulders inside her jacket in an attempt to become invisible. *He can't see me, can he?* she worried. No, not with all the trees, and the fountain. *OK, I'd better get ready. . . .*

Jeremy began pacing and checking his watch just as Jessica had been doing a few minutes earlier. No doubt about it; he was expecting someone. Jessica raised the camcorder, resting it on her knee for balance, and waited tensely.

At twenty-five minutes before nine o'clock, Sue dashed up, looking breathless. As Sue approached Jeremy, Jessica hit the power button and began filming. *A little closer,* she thought, peering through the viewfinder, *a little closer and I'll have what I came for. . . .*

Just as Jeremy spotted Sue and held out his arms to her, something knocked Jessica from behind. She fell forward, the baseball cap flying from her head and the camcorder tumbling from her hands. "What the . . . !"

"Oh, I'm so sorry!" Turning around, Jessica found herself glaring at a young mother with a toddler in her arms. The woman had bumped into Jessica with a stroller overloaded with shopping bags. "Are you OK? Did I hurt you?"

Bending, Jessica retrieved the video camera. "I'm fine," she muttered, glancing quickly across the courtyard. She wasn't hurt, but the moment was lost. Jeremy and Sue had disappeared into the crowd.

Standing up, Jessica tucked the camcorder into her shoulder bag and jammed the baseball cap back on her head. *I blew it,* she fumed silently as she stalked toward the exit. *Thanks to that dumb lady, they got away.*

By the time she reached the Jeep at the far end of the parking garage, Jessica's anger at the woman with the stroller had faded, and self-doubt had taken its place. *Did I blow it on purpose?* she couldn't help wondering. *I dropped the camera pretty fast . . . was I glad to have an excuse to turn away?*

It didn't really matter, Jessica decided glumly as

she turned the key in the ignition. She hadn't captured Jeremy and Sue on film, but she'd seen enough to know that Sue had been telling the truth.

Tears stung Jessica's eyes, and for a moment, before backing the Jeep out of the parking space, she folded her arms on the steering wheel and dropped her head. *I told Liz I was ready to face the truth,* she thought, letting the tears flow, *but maybe I don't really* want *to.*

Sue sat at the table in Jeremy's rented room, flipping through a newspaper. After meeting at Hampshire Place, they'd grabbed a quick bite to eat and then gone for a long walk on a misty, deserted stretch of beach. Now Jeremy was warming up with a hot shower, while she'd settled for a pot of tea.

Tossing the newspaper aside with a sigh, Sue cupped her hands around the mug and bent forward to breathe in the steam. Jeremy was being particularly sweet and attentive that evening . . . so why did she feel so restless, so unhappy? The sliver of doubt had buried itself too deeply in her heart to be dispelled. *When he holds me in his arms,* she thought, *and kisses me and tells me he loves me and that there's never been anyone else, it's all an act. It's all a lie. From the start, it's the money he's been in love with.*

Besides that, she was afraid of him—she was

afraid of the man she loved. Sue forced herself to acknowledge this, clenching her jaw to keep from crying. She couldn't trust Jeremy, and she was afraid of him. What kind of basis was that for a lifelong partnership?

Rising to her feet, Sue crossed the room to where Jeremy had dropped his clothes onto the bed. For a moment she stood listening. The shower was still running; it was safe. Quickly, she lifted Jeremy's pants, feeling in the pocket for his wallet. Removing it, she flipped it open and started thumbing through the contents. Credit card, driver's license, fifty dollars in cash, charge receipts from restaurants and gas stations, a Project Nature pay stub. Checking to see if there was anything else in Jeremy's pocket, Sue pulled out something that looked like a plane ticket.

A plane ticket? Sue raised her eyebrows. Had Jeremy already bought their tickets to New York? But they hadn't even finalized their plans for leaving Sweet Valley!

Unfolding the airline envelope, Sue removed the ticket. There was only one. She read the information printed on it: Jeremy Randall, one way from Los Angeles International to Hawaii and on to the South Pacific.

The flights were scheduled for the following Saturday. *One week from today,* Sue thought, the color draining from her face. Her knees buckled and she sat down on the bed. Saturday . . . the day they'd discussed flying to New York *together*. Instead, Jeremy was secretly planning to take off in the opposite direction . . . alone. What could it mean?

Quickly, Sue tucked the ticket back into its envelope. Sticking the envelope and the wallet back into Jeremy's pants pocket, she sprang to her feet, suddenly galvanized. *What else is he hiding from me?* she wondered, her eyes wild.

The shower was still running. Taking advantage of this, Sue began a rapid search of Jeremy's belongings. His briefcase was full of papers and notes relating to Project Nature—nothing out of the ordinary there. In his dresser drawers she found the expected jumble of clothing as well as an assortment of odds and ends: a few paperback novels, a book of matches from a Sweet Valley restaurant, a handful of coins, some unopened junk mail, and a plastic film canister. *Nothing,* Sue thought, clutching the film canister and trying to slow the pace of her pounding heart. *Maybe I'm overreacting. Maybe . . . maybe this isn't how it appears.*

She sank back down onto the bed, idly flipping the plastic cap off the canister. Instead of a roll of film, a newspaper clipping was hidden inside.

Sue unfolded the clipping and smoothed it out on the bedspread. Suddenly it felt as if the air had been sucked out of the room; she was having difficulty breathing. "A wedding announcement," she whispered. Accompanying the brief article was a photograph of the happy couple. She focused on the groom, feeling as if she might faint.

She recognized his face. The hair was darker, and he was a bit younger, but she'd know him anywhere. It was Jeremy!

The face was Jeremy's, but according to the newspaper article, the groom's name was Matt Thorn. *How can this be?* Sue wondered, pressing a trembling hand to her forehead. Jeremy had married someone else two years ago in Atlanta, under another name? *But Jeremy isn't Jeremy. He's Matt. Or maybe he's someone else altogether. What's going on?*

All at once Sue realized that the apartment was silent. The water had stopped running in the bathroom.

She jumped to her feet, on impulse stuffing the newspaper clipping into her pocket. Putting the cap back on the film canister, she returned it to the dresser drawer, hoping that Jeremy wouldn't be able to detect any signs of her snooping. She was getting a can of soda from the fridge when he emerged from the steamy bathroom, a towel tied around his waist.

He came up behind her and wrapped his arms around her. Sue stiffened. Before when Jeremy had touched her, she'd melted; now she found his nearness repulsive. But she had to hide her emotions; she didn't want to give any sign of her latest, most horrifying discovery.

120

"Our life is going to be perfect, do you know that?" Jeremy murmured, his breath warm against the back of her neck. "With your inheritance we can have everything we've ever wanted—go anywhere, do anything."

"It'll be a dream come true," Sue whispered.

He held her more tightly. "Just a few more days, and then nothing will part us, ever."

Sue thought about dark-haired Matt Thorn taking a bride in Atlanta. What had happened to *her*? "Nothing," she agreed, swallowing tears.

Moving away from her, Jeremy grabbed a can of beer from the refrigerator. "We're in the homestretch," he continued, his tone upbeat and confident, "but we've got to be more careful than ever. We can't afford to blow it when we're so close to getting out of here without anyone suspecting."

Sue thought about her confession to Jessica, and her lips tightened into a pale, thin line. "I'm being very careful," she said.

Jeremy nodded. "I know you are." He patted her cheek. "You've been terrific, Sue, just terrific. Still"—a frown creased his forehead—"keep your eyes and ears open for any sign that Jessica might be onto us."

Sue's stomach lurched. "Why—why do you say that?"

"She's been acting a little funny lately," he replied, taking a swig of the beer. "Blowing off dates, saying she's sick . . . I just hope for her sake it's some silly high-school problem."

Dread closed around Sue's heart like an icy fist. "What do you mean, for her sake?" she asked.

Jeremy leaned back against the kitchen counter. His posture was casual, but the expression in his eyes was cold, black, ruthless. "Nothing is going to come between me, I mean *us*, and that money," he declared. "Nothing."

"So if Jessica finds out what we're up to . . . ?"

He shrugged carelessly, finishing off the can of beer. "We'll have to get rid of her."

Without another glance at Sue, Jeremy strode back toward the bedroom to change. Now it was Sue's turn to lean against the counter, her body weak from shock and fear.

It was almost too much to absorb all at once. The one-way plane ticket, the newspaper clipping, Jeremy's threat against Jessica . . . *He never cared for me, even a tiny bit,* Sue realized, biting her lip until it bled. *Jeremy Randall probably isn't his real name—he's a liar, an impostor! Oh, how did I get myself into such a mess? And I've entangled and endangered Jessica, too. . . .*

Sue pressed her fingers against her forehead, wishing she could rub away the stress, the confusion, the fear. *I'm better off without him,* she thought. *I couldn't care less about that stupid money at this point—he can have it, he can have it all.* Easy enough to say—but after digging a hole so deep, how could she ever climb out now? If Jeremy thought for a minute that she was backing out, that he was going to lose the money . . .

Sue's face turned deathly pale. She pictured the one-way plane ticket; Jeremy's bald statement resounded in her brain. "Nothing's going to come between me and that money. We'll have to get rid of her. . . ."

Jeremy wants the money all to himself, and he'll stop at nothing—even murder, perhaps—to get it. Is he planning to get rid of me too?

"I'll try again with the video camera," Jessica offered gamely late Saturday night. "I'll stake out Jeremy's room in the boardinghouse. Maybe Sue visits him there."

Jessica had returned from her fruitless trip to Hampshire Place, and Elizabeth was home from the Beach Disco. Now the twins were sitting cross-legged on Elizabeth's bed, trying to come up with another plan for gathering hard evidence against Jeremy and Sue. Elizabeth shook her head at her sister's suggestion. "Maybe that's not the best idea after all," she decided. "It would be too easy for Jeremy to spot you, and then we'd be in big trouble."

"So what do we do, just let him and Sue get away with all that money?" Jessica declared, frustrated.

At that moment there was a soft knock on the bedroom door. "Who is it?" Elizabeth called.

"It's Sue."

The twins glanced at each other, surprised.

"Come on in," Elizabeth invited after a moment's hesitation.

The door swung open and Sue stepped into the room. Remembering that she was supposed to have a stomach flu, Jessica sank back against the pillows, trying to look tired and weak.

"What's up?" Elizabeth asked, flashing Sue a false smile.

Sue didn't return the smile; in fact, her expression was exceedingly somber.

"Sue, is something wrong?" Elizabeth inquired.

A horrible possibility occurred to Jessica. *They saw me at Hampshire Place—Jeremy knows I know!*

Sue pulled out Elizabeth's desk chair and took a seat. She crossed her legs and then her arms, clearly nervous. "I—I need to talk to you two about . . . about Jeremy," she stuttered.

Jessica nudged her twin with her foot, reminding Elizabeth that she wasn't supposed to know about Sue's confession two nights earlier. "What about Jeremy?" Elizabeth asked carefully.

"Oh, Elizabeth." Sue's eyes brimmed, and then the tears spilled over, streaming down her cheeks. "I told Jessica something the other night, something terrible, only now it turns out it's much, much worse. . . ."

"How could it be *worse?*" Jessica burst out.

"Sue, what's happened?" demanded Elizabeth.

Sue wiped her eyes on her sleeve. "Oh, Liz, I

can't bear for you to know what a nasty person I am," she sobbed. "It was hard enough telling Jessica, and I . . . I just can't . . ."

"She knows," Jessica said.

Sue looked up. "What?" she gasped.

"Elizabeth knows," Jessica repeated. "I told her. I had to tell somebody."

"But that's good!" Sue cried, to Jessica's surprise. "Oh, I'm *glad* she knows. Now the three of us can go after Jeremy together!"

Both Elizabeth and Jessica stared at Sue as if she'd gone stark raving mad. "Wait a minute," said Elizabeth. "The three of us go after Jeremy? I was under the impression you and Jeremy were a team, Sue."

"I know I've behaved despicably," Sue said, leaning forward in the chair with earnest, pleading eyes. "But you have to believe me when I say I'm on your side now."

The twins exchanged a skeptical glance. "I don't trust her," Jessica hissed in Elizabeth's ear. Out loud she asked Sue, "Why this sudden turnaround?"

"I found . . ." Sue gulped; obviously this was hard for her to say. "I found a plane ticket in a pocket of Jeremy's pants. A one-way ticket to the South Pacific. I thought we were going to fly to New York together after the money was transferred to my account, but apparently he has a secret plan of his own. A plan to take the money and then abandon me or even . . . maybe even kill me," she choked out.

Elizabeth's eyebrows shot up. "You have to help me," Sue continued, her voice barely audible, "and you have to let me help you. I'll do whatever it takes, even if it means turning myself in. We've got to bring Jeremy to justice."

Jessica kicked Elizabeth again. She mouthed the same words. "I don't trust her. . . ."

"Why should we believe you?" Elizabeth asked. "I mean, face it, Sue, you haven't been truthful about one thing since you came to Sweet Valley. How do we know you're not lying about this? For all we know, you've decided Jeremy's a jerk and you're just trying to get him in trouble so you don't have to share your inheritance with him."

"Yeah, show us the plane ticket, and then maybe we'll have something to talk about," Jessica contributed.

"I can't show you the plane ticket," said Sue, "but I can show you this." Reaching into her jacket pocket, she pulled out a folded piece of newspaper, which she handed to Elizabeth.

Elizabeth unfolded the clipping while Jessica looked over her shoulder. "'Matt Thorn and Marla Tannenbaum wed in Atlanta,'" Elizabeth read out loud.

"Oh, my gosh." Jessica clapped a hand to her mouth. "The picture. Liz, look."

Elizabeth stared at the black-and-white photo. "It looks like . . . but it can't be . . ."

"It's Jeremy," Jessica cried. "Matt Thorn is Jeremy Randall!"

"Now do you believe me?" asked Sue quietly.

Elizabeth stared at Sue. "He's a con artist!"

"I'd bet anything he married Marla Tannenbaum for her money, and that's what he's trying to do with me," Sue confirmed.

Jessica shuddered. Sue was right—this *was* even worse. Jeremy was not only selfish, greedy, and cruel; he was a hardened criminal intending to pull off a half-million-dollar heist. And it probably wasn't the first time.

Elizabeth rubbed her arms, which prickled with goose bumps. "The money becomes yours on Wednesday, Sue, but obviously Jeremy expects it to be his alone when he leaves the country on Saturday. What kind of twisted plan is he hatching?"

The three girls looked at each other, their faces identical masks of dread. Only one thing was certain. The web of intrigue and terror was tightening. They were in much deeper than they ever imagined.

Chapter 9

On Sunday, Elizabeth had had a brainstorm, which she couldn't pursue because the high-school building was locked. It was torture to wait until Monday morning, but there wasn't any other choice.

Now, at seven A.M. on Monday, Elizabeth, Jessica, and Sue walked into Sweet Valley High and made a beeline for the *Oracle* office. "I'm almost afraid of what we might find," Sue confided in a low voice as Elizabeth unlocked the office door with her key.

"We need to learn more about Matt Thorn," Elizabeth reminded her. The lock clicked and she pushed the door open. "If we want to nail Jeremy . . ."

At such an early hour, they had the newspaper office to themselves. Elizabeth got right to business, quickly sitting down in front of one of the computers and switching on the power. "It takes a minute to boot up," she informed Jessica and Sue, who were pacing impatiently. She watched the screen intently, then beckoned the other two over. "OK. We're ready to start!"

Jessica and Sue crowded close so they could see over Elizabeth's shoulder as she accessed INFO-MAX and typed in the name "Matt Thorn." All three held their breath; the atmosphere pulsed with suspense.

It didn't take long for the computer to locate all existing references to Matt Thorn. "There's only one newspaper article about him!" Jessica exclaimed.

Elizabeth hit a few more keys, and the article appeared on the screen.

"It's the same one I found in Jeremy's drawer," observed Sue. "The wedding announcement in the Atlanta paper."

"So this was all for nothing." Jessica sighed, disappointed. "We didn't learn anything."

"On the contrary." Elizabeth turned to Sue and Jessica, her eyes flashing. "Don't you see? This is the *only* story that's ever been printed about Matt Thorn. That in itself tells us a lot about him!"

Sue's eyes glinted with comprehension. "You're right."

Jessica wrinkled her forehead. "I still don't get it."

"Matt Thorn never really existed," Sue explained to Jessica. "Or rather, Jeremy must have

129

created that identity solely for the purpose of duping this Marla Tannenbaum, whoever she is." A shadow darkened Sue's face. "Just like he probably created the identity of Jeremy Randall just for the purpose of conning *me*."

"For all we know, he has other aliases," said Elizabeth, turning back to the computer. "Let's see what INFOMAX has to say about Marla Tannenbaum."

The computer produced quite a list of references about Matt Thorn's bride. Elizabeth pulled up the first article. "She was a debutante in Atlanta a couple of years ago," she read. "Looks like she's from a pretty prominent family."

"A real socialite—and an heiress," remarked Sue as they perused a few more stories about Marla. "Well, that explains Jeremy's—or rather Matt's—interest in her."

"It's all making sense," Elizabeth agreed.

"I wonder whatever happened between Matt and Marla," said Jessica. "I mean, we know he's not still with her because he's here in Sweet Valley being Jeremy Randall. You don't suppose . . ." Her eyes widened. "You don't suppose he *killed* her."

"Of course not," said Elizabeth, "or there'd be a notice about her death. No, I don't think that's Jeremy's style."

"There's one way to find out," said Sue suddenly.

"To find out about what?" asked Elizabeth.

"About Matt and Marla." Sue's eyes glittered. "We could ask Marla herself!"

Jessica gaped. "You mean, like, *call* her?"

Sue nodded. "What do we have to lose?"

The issue decided, the three girls hurried back out into the corridor. A few students had drifted in, but for the most part, the school was still quiet. "There's no one over by the pay phone," Elizabeth observed as they crossed the lobby. "Here goes nothing!"

She dialed the operator and asked for the area code in Atlanta, then dialed Atlanta information. "Do you have a number for Marla Tannenbaum?" she asked, expecting to be told that it was unlisted. To her surprise a computer-generated voice said, "The number is . . ."

Elizabeth gestured wildly. Seizing the pen Sue handed her, Elizabeth printed the phone number on the back of her left hand. "I've got it!"

She hung up the phone and looked from Sue to Jessica. "OK, who wants to be the one to call Marla?"

Jessica volunteered. "I will."

Sue was nibbling her fingernails. "What are you going to say to her? What if she hangs up on us? What if—"

"She won't hang up on me," Jessica said confidently. "Just watch."

Using Sue's long-distance calling card, Jessica punched in Marla Tannenbaum's Atlanta phone number. A few tense seconds passed, and then she said in a very businesslike voice, "Hello, may I speak with Ms. Marla Tannenbaum, please?"

An instant later Jessica cupped her hand over the mouthpiece. "It's her!" she whispered excitedly to Elizabeth and Sue.

Elizabeth held her breath, wondering what on earth Jessica planned to say to Ms. Tannenbaum. *We should have rehearsed something,* she thought anxiously. *We can't afford to blow this lead. . . .*

She shouldn't have worried; Jessica handled the situation like a seasoned private eye. "Ms. Tannenbaum, this is Detective Belsky of the Sweet Valley, California, police force," she said briskly. "We're investigating a kidnapping case and have reason to believe you might know something about the whereabouts of our chief suspect, a twenty-three-year-old man by the name of Matt Thorn."

Clearly, Marla Tannenbaum had something to say on the subject. For a few minutes Jessica did nothing but nod. "So you never filed charges against him, and you haven't yet filed for a divorce?" she said at last. Another minute passed. "Thank you very much for your time, Ms. Tannenbaum. You've been very helpful."

Jessica replaced the phone, a look of grim amusement on her face. "What did she say? What did she say?" Elizabeth and Sue chorused.

"It's pretty much what we expected," Jessica told them. "According to Marla, she met Matt two years ago, and they were married after a whirlwind courtship. She didn't know much about him, but he was charming, handsome, devoted. He seemed to be interested in all the same social causes she cared about, and they talked about spending their life together working on philanthropic projects." Jessica shot a quick glance at Sue, who flushed unhappily. "Right after their wedding he talked her into putting a huge piece of her fortune in a foundation for their future philanthropic work. The money was in both their names . . . and he stole it all."

"All of it?" Sue squeaked.

"All of it. Then he disappeared without a trace. She never heard from him again."

Sue leaned against the wall next to the pay phone, her face white as chalk. Elizabeth pressed Jessica for more details. "Why didn't we see anything about that on INFOMAX?"

"Marla said she was just too humiliated to go public with the story," answered Jessica. "Her family's kept the whole thing under tight wraps."

"Wow." Elizabeth exhaled. "What a scam!"

"I don't understand." Sue clasped her hands tightly, her knuckles whitening. "If he took all that money from Marla, why does he need *my* money?"

"He's a career criminal," speculated Elizabeth. "Maybe he spent Marla's money, or maybe he just wants *more* money. Because of your expected inheritance, you were a likely target, but if it hadn't been you . . . it probably would have been someone else."

Sue hung her head. "I feel like the world's biggest fool," she whispered. "I can understand why Marla didn't want anyone to know what she let him do to her."

"So where do we go from here?" Jessica asked.

Elizabeth frowned, thinking hard. "I guess . . . I guess we wait for Jeremy to make the next move."

"Which will happen sometime between Wednesday and Saturday," Sue predicted, "the day I get my inheritance, and the date on his plane ticket."

"We have to be on our guard," stated Elizabeth. "All of us, but especially you two. There's a lot at stake for Jeremy . . . or Matt or whoever he is. He's a dangerous man. And in the meantime, we have to keep up the charade if we don't want him to suspect that we're on his trail."

"The charade?" said Sue.

Elizabeth nodded. "It's up to you and Jess." The other two girls looked at each other, their faces pale and grim. "That's right," said Elizabeth. "You both have to pretend that you're still in love with Jeremy Randall."

Jessica slouched into the kitchen at home, dropping her backpack on the floor just inside the door. For some reason cheerleading practice had wiped her out—she felt as if she'd just run a marathon. *That's because I haven't been sleeping much lately*, she thought, automatically reaching for the door to the refrigerator. *Ever since my life turned into a nightmare* . . .

The long white florist's box on the counter stopped her in her tracks. Curious, Jessica checked the name on the card taped to the lid. "They're for me!" she exclaimed out loud.

She opened the box eagerly. Inside, two dozen long-stemmed red roses nestled in green tissue paper, their buds tightly closed and perfect. Closing her eyes, Jessica inhaled the heavenly scent. *Red roses, my absolute favorite,* she thought, picking up the envelope and examining the handwriting. *Who could have* . . .

As she slid the card from the envelope, the flush of pleasure faded from her cheeks. Of course. The flowers were from Jeremy.

"Dear Jessica," the card read, "you made it to school today, so you must be feeling better. I hope tonight will be the night. . . . All my love, Jeremy."

I hope tonight will be the night. . . . The card slipped from Jessica's fingers. Pressing a hand to her mouth, she fought back the urge to vomit. Suddenly, the sweet perfume of the roses seemed overpowering, sickening, and when she looked down at the gorgeous flowers, all she could see was their cruel thorns. *Matt Thorn,* Jessica thought. Like the roses, Jeremy Randall's appearance was deceptive. *What a perfect name for him to choose.* . . .

Shoving the lid back on, Jessica grabbed the

florist's box and sprinted for the door. Jogging over to the house next door, she leaned hard on the bell. Mrs. Beckwith answered the door. "Jessica, is anything wrong?" she asked when she saw Jessica's panting, disturbed expression.

Jessica shook her head. "No, but we got these roses and I'm . . . I'm allergic. Achew!" She faked a sneeze. "I thought you might like them." She shoved the box into Mrs. Beckwith's hands. "Here, they're yours."

Turning, Jessica started back toward her own house. "Why, thank you, dear," Mrs. Beckwith called after her.

Back in the kitchen, Jessica slumped against the counter, her head in her hands. The roses were gone, but their scent still lingered in the air. And there was Jeremy's card lying on the floor. . . .

Picking up the card, Jessica forced herself to read its message one more time before tearing it up and throwing it into the trash. She remembered Elizabeth's words to her that morning in the lobby before school. "We have to keep up the charade . . . you have to go on pretending that you're in love with Jeremy. . . ."

Jessica counted to ten slowly in her head and then reached for the phone mounted on the wall. After counting to ten again, she dialed Jeremy's number.

He picked up after the first ring. "Hello?"

"Jeremy, it's Jessica."

"Jessica! It's so good to hear your voice. I've missed you so much."

Jessica swallowed, once again fighting down nausea. "I—I've missed you, too," she lied. "Thanks for the roses—they're beautiful."

"Not as beautiful as you," he said gallantly, "but then, nothing and no one is."

"You . . . you're just too sweet."

"So you sound better," he observed. "Can I see you?"

Jessica's hand tightened on the phone. She wanted nothing more than to tell Jeremy she was still sick, she couldn't go out, she'd never be able to see him again. But she'd run out of excuses. She couldn't keep putting him off without making him suspicious. "Yeah, you can see me," she said somewhat hoarsely.

"Let me take you out tonight," he offered.

"Tonight would be . . . great."

"I'll pick you up at six. And, Jessica . . ."

"Yeah?"

"I love you."

"I—I love you, too."

She hung up the phone. Her hand was shaking; her whole body was shaking. "Stop it," she said out loud to herself. "Just stop it." She knew she had to get herself under control. She had to be on her toes tonight when she went out with Jeremy—she had to be thinking fast, had to be cool and collected. She couldn't afford to let him get the upper hand, not even for a minute. . . .

"I wish you could find a way to get out of it," Elizabeth said to Jessica.

Jessica turned away from her closet to face her sister. "You think I'm looking forward to this? The thought of being alone with him . . ." She shuddered.

"Promise you won't go with him to the beach or anyplace too isolated," Elizabeth begged. "Stick to public places—a restaurant, the movies. And if he tries anything, just get out of there."

If he tries anything . . . Jessica pretended to thumb through some shirts and skirts, hiding her face from Elizabeth. *What would Liz say if she knew that Jeremy and I had been planning to sleep together, and that he probably still assumes I'm interested?*

Elizabeth wasn't ready to give up on talking Jessica out of keeping her date with Jeremy. "Why not tell him you've had a relapse of the stomach flu?" she suggested. "Or you have a test tomorrow in school, or—"

"Didn't you say yourself that I have to keep up the charade?" Jessica countered. She laughed humorlessly. "And since when have I ever canceled a date because of homework?"

Elizabeth managed a half-smile. "Yeah, I guess that *would* be out of character."

"I can handle Jeremy," Jessica said, though without much conviction. "Here, which dress?"

She held up two dresses, a sleeveless navy-blue knit dress with an elastic waist and a scoop neck, and a loose, casual bright-orange T-shirt dress. They were probably the least sexy of Jessica's wardrobe, but they were both short. "Don't you have anything longer?" asked Elizabeth, frowning at the above-the-knee hemlines.

"What were we just saying about staying in character?" Jessica said somewhat impatiently. "I can't suddenly start dressing as boring as . . ." She thought of the least fashionable person she knew. "Enid Rollins." Elizabeth stuck out her tongue. "Just help me decide, OK? Which dress?"

Twenty minutes later it was six o'clock, and the early-winter sun was just setting. Wearing the navy dress, a wheat-colored linen jacket, sandals, and very little makeup, Jessica paced the living room, waiting for Jeremy. *Maybe something will come up and he'll have to cancel,* she thought hopefully, fidgeting with the gold lavaliere she wore on a delicate chain around her neck. *Maybe he'll have car trouble, or maybe* he'll *get the stomach flu, for real.*

As she looked out the window, she saw headlights approaching the driveway. The car slowed, and then the driver tapped his horn. It was Jeremy.

The waitress at the Cypress Point Cafe cleared their plates. "That was delicious," Jessica

139

said to Jeremy, even though she'd managed to swallow only a few bites of her dinner. "I love this restaurant."

"I think of it as our special place," he said, a meaningful look in his eyes. Reaching across the table, he clasped Jessica's hand, playing with the diamond-and-sapphire engagement ring on her fourth finger. "Remember the last time we were here?"

She nodded, her skin crawling at his touch.

"We talked about finding time to be alone together." She tried to withdraw her hand from his, but he only squeezed it more tightly. "What do you think about that now?"

"I think . . ." Jessica looked around for the waitress, panic stealing into her heart. *I've got to get out of here.* . . . "I think we should ask for the check."

To her dismay Jeremy grinned widely. "My sentiments exactly."

Oh, no, Jessica thought, biting back a whimper. *He took that the wrong way! I'd better clear up this misunderstanding fast, or I'm in trouble.*

Jeremy settled the check and then escorted Jessica from the restaurant, one arm solid and heavy around her shoulders. In the parking lot he turned her body to face his and pressed her close for a long, aggressive kiss.

Finally, Jessica managed to pull away, breathless and trying desperately to hide her repulsion.

"So what do you say we go to that condo by the beach I was telling you about?" said Jeremy. "My friend's still out of town—we'll have it all to ourselves. . . ."

"I actually . . . I can't," Jessica stuttered. "I have a ton of homework—I got really behind because of being sick."

"Homework?" Jeremy raised his eyebrows at Jessica, who was already climbing into the passenger seat of his rental car. "You're kidding. It can't wait until tomorrow?"

She shook her head. "I have to make up a couple of quizzes, and I'm way behind on my reading. It's almost finals, and I could—I could flunk math if I don't make up the assignments I missed," she lied.

Jeremy started the car. "But we've been planning this, Jessica." Twisting in the seat, he stared straight into her eyes. "Did something happen? Have you changed your mind?"

She stared back at him, praying her fear wasn't visible. "Of course not," she said, forcing herself to put a hand on his arm and stroke his skin. "I haven't changed my mind—far from it."

He seemed mollified. "Then let's just stop by the condo for an hour or so." He grinned. "I'll give you something to think about while you're studying."

"No, let's . . . let's wait till a night when we're not rushed." Jessica mustered up the ghost of a flirtatious smile; she put a teasing note in her voice. "The longer we wait, the better it'll be, right?"

A hot light flickered in Jeremy's eyes. "Right. But let's not wait *too* long, baby."

Because you're planning to love me and leave me, you big jerk! Jessica thought.

The instant Jeremy pulled up at the curb in front of her house, Jessica shoved open the passenger-side door and swung one leg from the car. The clean getaway she'd hoped for was thwarted by Jeremy, however. Pulling her back into the car, he assaulted her with repulsive good-bye kisses. "Don't make me wait too long," he repeated in a husky voice when she finally managed to tear herself from his arms.

Not trusting herself to reply, Jessica blew him one last kiss and raced to the house. She wasn't sure she was going to make it inside before bursting into tears. As upset and revolted as she felt, though, she couldn't help seeing the frightful irony in the situation. *Not long ago I thought Jeremy Randall was the most attractive guy on earth*, she recalled.

She'd been ready to marry him, but now Jeremy Randall made her sick. He was the enemy.

Chapter 10

When the bell rang signaling the beginning of lunch period on Wednesday, Jessica dragged her feet down the hall in the direction of the cafeteria. Colorful posters advertising Friday's Mistletoe Madness dance stared at her from every wall, heartless reminders that she was never going to be able to get into the holiday spirit this season—and that she didn't have a date for the dance because her fiancé had turned out to be a professional con artist and crook.

Feeling more than a little sorry for herself, she loaded up her lunch tray with food she didn't really have an appetite for and skirted the crowd to sit by herself at a small corner table. Her shoulders slumped, she picked apathetically at the sandwich, the bowl of soup, the bag of chips, and then shoved the tray away. Nothing had any flavor.

I wonder what Sue's doing right now. Leaning

her elbows on the table, Jessica rested her chin in her hands. Today was the day the inheritance was supposed to be transferred into Sue's New York bank account. Jeremy was probably bugging Sue to find out if the money came through. Would he try to persuade her to take some of it out for him right away? How was he planning to get his hands on all of it before Saturday?

Jessica sighed heavily. *I can't even hate Sue anymore,* she realized, disgruntled. *I have to feel sorry for her because Jeremy fooled her even worse than he fooled me. We're both idiots—he never loved either of us! Boy, Wakefield, you really know how to pick 'em. When did you turn into such a loser?*

Her depressing train of thought was interrupted by a movement in front of her face. Jessica blinked, focusing, and saw that someone had reached from behind her to place a single white rose next to her lunch tray.

Twisting in her chair, Jessica looked up into Ken's smiling face. "Ken! What—it's beautiful, but why . . . ?"

"You just look so sad today," he said with a shrug. "I thought this might cheer you up a little."

He was blushing slightly, and now Jessica's face reddened, too. She hated to be caught off guard, with her emotions totally on display. "Oh, no, I'm fine," she hurried to assure Ken, flashing her breeziest, most carefree smile. "Maybe a little tired, that's all. But thanks anyhow—"

Having given her a quick wave, Ken was already melting back into the lunchroom crowd. Jessica looked after him for a minute, a trace of a smile still lingering on her bemused face. *Of course, they don't know the whole story, but maybe Lila and Amy have been spreading it around that Jeremy and I are breaking up,* she surmised. It was a little embarrassing to have Ken feeling sorry for her, but at the same time, his gesture warmed her inside. Glancing down, Jessica touched the single, beautiful rose. Someone—Ken?—had carefully plucked off all the thorns, leaving only the pure, fragrant flower. Jessica lifted it to her face, breathing in the perfume. *I'll keep this one,* she thought, remembering how desperate she'd been to get rid of Jeremy's ostentatious bouquet. In contrast, Ken's white rose really did smell sweet.

"Ken did what? A rose?" Lila jingled her car keys as she spoke on the phone with Jessica after school on Wednesday. "You're kidding. Well, yeah, Amy and I probably did hint that you and Jeremy were going to call off your engagement. Ken really works fast, huh? Oh, come on—why else would he buy you flowers? OK, I don't have time to argue with you—it doesn't mean anything, Ken's just Mr. Sensitive. I'm on my way to the gallery for the opening. Wish me luck!"

Returning the cordless phone to its rest, Lila

smoothed the skirt of her elegant raw-silk suit and then dashed for the door. She couldn't wait to get to the gallery and hang her paintings. It occurred to her that if the pictures were a hit, not only would Robby's career be salvaged, but she'd be launching her own career. *An artist—I never thought about that possibility,* she mused. *But why not? Robby and I could spend our lives traveling around Europe with our easels. Fun!*

The ten paintings, still in their cartons, were leaning like dominoes in one corner of the gallery office. Lila had scrawled Robby's name all over the boxes before having her father's chauffeur deliver them. Strolling confidently across the office, Lila held out her hand to introduce herself to Mrs. DeForest, the gallery owner.

"Hi, Mrs. DeForest, I'm Lila Fowler, Robby's . . ." She hesitated for a split second. Robby's girlfriend? "Robby's agent."

"Oh. I wasn't expecting . . ." Mrs. DeForest arched carefully plucked auburn eyebrows, looking mildly surprised. "Well, it's nice to meet you, Lila."

"I'll be setting up the paintings. Could you show me where you want them to go?"

"Of course." Mrs. DeForest gestured with a slender arm weighted down by heavy silver-and-turquoise bracelets. "The other artists are already up, but there's a wall waiting just for him."

Carrying one of the boxes, Lila followed Mrs. DeForest into the gallery, eyeballing Robby's competition. One artist had done some pretty watercolors. *Tame, totally ordinary,* Lila thought dismissively. *And those abstract seascapes? I could do better in my sleep!* She couldn't suppress a smug smile. Her paintings were definitely more colorful and more dramatic—altogether bolder and newer. *I'm—I mean, Robby's—going to be the hit of the show!*

Standing in front of a blank wall studded with picture hooks, Mrs. DeForest waited with clasped hands as Lila slid the first painting from the box. "Robby calls this one 'Harbor,'" announced Lila, turning it so Mrs. DeForest could see.

The gallery owner's jaw dropped. "Oh, my, I—" She put a hand to her mouth. "Well. I've seen a number of Robby's pieces, and I expected something . . ."

Her sentence trailed off into mystified silence. *She's stunned. She thinks it's good!* Lila beamed. "The use of color is arresting, don't you think?" she asked, hoping she sounded like an art agent.

"Arresting . . . yes," Mrs. DeForest agreed somewhat doubtfully.

"And the composition." Lila studied the painting with affection. "Quite revolutionary, wouldn't you say?"

Mrs. DeForest winced. "Umm."

In a few minutes all ten paintings were hung. As Mrs. DeForest positioned a printed card with Robby's name on it and a short biography of the artist, Lila stepped back to admire the whole effect. "Wow," she murmured, blinking in admiration. "They look pretty darned good, if I may say so myself!"

"Well, thanks for your help, Lila," Mrs. DeForest said as she, too, cast a last uncertain look at Robby's portion of the exhibit. "I'm just going to run into the next room to see if my assistant has the wine and cheese ready. The guests should start arriving any minute."

Fifteen minutes later the first handful of guests arrived at the door to the gallery, where they were greeted by Mrs. DeForest and Martin Lake, her assistant. Chewing her lip nervously, Lila glanced at her watch. *Where's Robby?* she wondered. Suddenly a terrible thought struck her. What if he wasn't planning to show up? *Of course*, she realized, sinking onto an upholstered bench near the wine-and-cheese table. It would be too humiliating to arrive empty-handed, to let down Mrs. DeForest and all the guests.

There wasn't a moment to lose. Jumping up again, Lila darted into Mrs. DeForest's office and rapidly dialed Robby's number on the desk phone. She'd tell him just to come to the gallery, that she'd taken care of everything, and then when he arrived and realized what she'd done for him . . . *He'll love me forever*, Lila thought with satisfaction.

There was no one home. "Shoot," muttered Lila, banging down the phone. "Why didn't I deal with this possibility sooner? I'll have to think up some excuse to tell Mrs. DeForest. . . ."

Hurrying out of the office, she saw that the gallery was now filled with guests already sampling the wine and cheese. By far the largest and most animated cluster of people was positioned in front of Robby's work, Lila was gratified to discover. One man was waving his arms; a few other people were pointing and exclaiming. *They love him!* Lila thought triumphantly.

Trying to appear sophisticated and nonchalant, she strolled toward Robby's paintings, primed to bask in the praise that was being tossed about. She wanted to memorize every glowing word so she could tell Robby all about it later.

As she approached the group, Lila caught snatches of their remarks.

". . . atrocious," a woman in a black beret declared.

". . . lifeless as mud," snorted the man standing next to her.

". . . reminiscent of bird droppings, perhaps," someone else proclaimed disdainfully.

". . . displays no technique whatsoever . . ."

". . . clearly the work of an undisciplined amateur . . ."

". . . you know what they say, for some people the first show is also the last show . . ."

". . . laughable!"

The color drained from Lila's warmly tanned cheeks. She put a hand to her throat, suddenly

feeling choked and dizzy. *They don't love him—
they hate him. Oh, my God, what have I done?*

"You don't understand," Lila protested, hurrying forward to argue the merits of the paintings.
"You have to appreciate the—"

At that moment the door flew open and someone burst into the gallery. Lila whirled along with
the others in time to see Robby flash a shy smile
at the assembled crowd. "Sorry I'm late," he said
to Mrs. DeForest. His eyes lit up as he spotted
Lila; she hunched her shoulders, wishing she
could sink into the floor. "I hope I haven't kept
everybody . . ."

His words were lost in the sound of people
whispering and laughing. "That's him . . ." "Nice-
looking boy, but about as much talent as a . . ."
"Well, at least he's young—lots of time to find another career!"

"You're not late at all," Mrs. DeForest informed
Robby, her smile somewhat stiff. "Your agent arrived in time to hang the paintings, so we've had a
chance already to form our opinions. . . ."

"My agent?" Robby's brow furrowed. "But I
don't—" Puzzled, he walked forward, his eyes dart-
ing from side to side. "I don't understand. How
could you hang my paintings when—"

His eyes fell on the placard with his name on
it and then moved quickly to the paintings on the
wall. The guests had shrunk back so he had a
clear view of Lila's creations, and what he saw

150

caused his eyes to bulge in their sockets. "What on earth . . . ?"

Lila stepped forward as if she were going to the guillotine, a mournful expression on her face. When Robby turned to stare at her, she lifted one limp hand. "Hi, Robby," she said sheepishly. "It's me, your agent . . . remember?"

Sue picked up the telephone in Mr. Wakefield's study. Glancing at the number listed on a recent statement, she dialed her bank in New York City. It was after business hours on the East Coast; a recorded message instructed her to use the touch-tone phone buttons to type in her account number and password in order to request information about her balance. Sue complied and then waited anxiously. After what seemed an age, the computer-generated voice recited an amount in dollars and cents. The flock of butterflies in Sue's stomach took rapid, disturbed flight.

The money wasn't there.

Sue hung up the phone. She'd called New York twice that morning, and both times bank representatives had assured her that the electronic transfer had taken place as scheduled—her balance would reflect the deposit by the end of the workday. Home for lunch, Mrs. Wakefield had cheerfully congratulated Sue on her inheritance. Now Wednesday was over and the money was missing in action. Where could it be?

❅   ❅   ❅

Lila stood in the parking lot behind the art gallery with her ten paintings, sobbing uncontrollably. One by one, she heaved the canvases into the trash, taking bitter pleasure in the crashing, crumpling sound they made as they hit the bottom of the Dumpster. "Lila Fowler, you are such a meddlesome idiot!" she cursed herself, kicking one of the paintings with the toe of her suede Italian pump. "You've ruined Robby's career—everybody's laughing at him, and he's never going to speak to you again. And if he decides to sue you for defamation of character or something, it will serve you right!"

Suddenly Lila realized through her tears that someone was standing beside her, trying to get her attention. "Lila, hey. It's OK. Calm down for a minute."

It was Robby. Lila dashed a hand across her damp eyes, sniffling. "Did you come out here to tell me you hate me?"

He smiled at her, his eyes warm with affection and remorse. "I'm sorry I got a little ticked off in there, but I was . . . well, you really threw me for a loop, Li. For a minute or two things were looking pretty grim. It was hard to grasp that you were trying to do me a favor—it looked more like sabotage!"

Lila burst into tears again. "Oh, Robby," she wailed, "can you ever forgive me?"

152

"Ssh." He wrapped his arms around her, pressing her against his chest. "There's nothing to forgive."

"I thought you didn't have any paintings of your own to show." Lila hiccuped. "I just wanted to help."

"It was kind of a misguided plan, but your heart was in the right place," said Robby.

Lila noticed his grin. "What are you laughing at?" she asked, frowning through her tears. "There's nothing funny about this situation, if you ask me."

"Come inside, I want to show you something."

Robby took Lila's hand. "No way!" She dug her heels into the pavement. "They'll just tear us to shreds. Let's get out of here, and you can start over at being an artist. You might have to move to another state, but I swear, I won't ever interfere with your career, ever again—"

"Just come inside," Robby repeated, dragging her back toward the gallery.

Reluctantly, Lila followed Robby inside. The gallery's patrons and the other artists were still milling about. When Lila and Robby reappeared, all conversation stopped. Lila turned beet-red, waiting for the laughter to begin.

To her surprise, instead of laughing, everyone burst into spontaneous applause.

"What are they clapping about?" Lila asked Robby in confusion.

Without speaking he led her over to the wall where, only a few minutes before, her paintings

had hung. In their place were ten new paintings—
ten paintings Lila had never laid eyes on before—
ten marvelous paintings.

"But what . . . !" Lila exclaimed, astonished.
"Robby, are they yours?"

He nodded proudly. "What do you think?"

Lila gazed at the paintings in awe. Like her,
Robby had painted a harbor scene, but instead of
being muddy and muddled, his canvas was a wash of
color, light, and movement. Impressionistic sailboats
skittered across the sea, chased by the shadow of an
oncoming storm. Then there was a series of Sweet
Valley storefronts, and some portraits of people in a
park: two old men reading newspapers on a bench,
children flying a kite, a row of surfboards on the sand.

The last painting was of a beautiful dark-haired
girl with coffee-brown eyes. Lila blushed furiously.
"Oh, Robby, they're . . . they're . . ."

"Some of the loveliest paintings I've had the
pleasure of exhibiting in a long time," said Mrs.
DeForest. "Let's toast this talented new artist, shall
we?" she invited the assembled crowd.

All around the room, glasses were raised.
Putting his arm around her waist, Robby gazed
down into Lila's eyes as the compliments flowed
over them.

Lila still couldn't believe her eyes. "But how—
when . . . ?" She and Robby stepped aside, out of
earshot of the gallery's guests. "But I never saw any
of these when I dropped by your studio! I thought

you were panicking about the opening and not getting any work done."

"I was in a panic," Robby admitted, "but it was a pretty productive panic. I was really nervous, though, and unsure of myself. I just couldn't bring myself to show any of this stuff to you. What if you didn't like it? I would've been crushed—I never would have picked up a paintbrush again." He smiled ruefully. "I wanted so much to impress you, for you to believe in me."

"But I do believe in you!" Lila declared. "I think you're the most wonderful, talented person in the world. I know I get pushy sometimes, but it's only because . . . well, because I always think I know what's best for people."

"I guess we've both learned that we need to trust each other more," Robby concluded.

Lila nodded, her eyes shining. "I'm so proud of you, Robby."

Bending, he kissed her lightly on the lips. "I'm glad you're here to share this moment with me."

"I want to share *every* moment with you, Robby."

"Speaking of which"—his eyes twinkled—"what's this I hear about a Mistletoe Madness dance? You still looking for a date?"

Lila flung her arms around his neck. "Nope. I've got a date already—I'm going to the dance with the West Coast's hottest new artist!"

Chapter 11

When Sue hung up the phone after speaking with Jeremy Wednesday night, her forehead was creased. He wasn't worried enough, she reflected, puzzled. The money was what Jeremy was after, right? So if there was some glitch with it, he should really be in a sweat. Instead, he had sounded almost careless.

Of course. I should've known. Sue's brow cleared and a grim smile twisted her lips. *If Jeremy's not worried about the money, then that's because he knows where it is. He must have already stolen it!*

Sue darted into the hallway. The twins' bedroom doors were both closed; she knocked loudly on Elizabeth's and then burst into the room without waiting for an invitation.

The twins were sitting cross-legged on the floor sorting through a pile of CDs. They looked up, startled by Sue's dramatic entrance. "OK, he's done it," Sue announced. "He stole my inheritance—he pulled off some stunt at the bank. Now we can go after him!"

Jessica and Elizabeth jumped to their feet. "What are you talking about?" Elizabeth cried.

"What's going on?" Jessica demanded.

Quickly, Sue filled them in on her frustrating day of unproductive phone calls to the bank in New York; then she recounted her conversation with Jeremy and his nonchalant response. "It's definitely fishy," Elizabeth agreed.

"He's got his hands on the money, all right," said Sue. "It follows, doesn't it? He stole Marla Tannenbaum's fortune, and obviously he's been planning all along to steal mine. He wasn't about to leave anything to chance—that's why he could buy that plane ticket ahead of time. He's ready to split."

"We have to stop him!" Jessica declared. "He can't get away with this."

Elizabeth calculated. "If he's planning to leave on Saturday, we only have forty-eight hours."

"Maybe it's time to go to the police again," suggested Jessica.

"We have to make sure we've really got him, though," said Elizabeth. "Remember what happened last time?"

"I want to catch him in the act," said Sue. "He's too smart—if the evidence isn't rock solid, he'll find a way to slime out of this. I want him punished."

Elizabeth directed a solemn gaze at Sue. "You know what that means, don't you, Sue?" she asked quietly. "If we prove Jeremy's guilty . . ."

"Then I'm guilty, too." Sue nodded, her jaw clenched. "I know I'm going to have to face up to the consequences of my actions. I'm ready."

"OK, then." Elizabeth beckoned to the other two girls to come closer. "Tell me what you think of this plan. . . ."

Jessica lay on her bed staring up at the ceiling. Even though it was a cool night, her forehead was beaded with sweat. *I've always wanted to be an actress,* she thought, mustering a smile as she recalled her various roles in Sweet Valley High dramatic productions and the time she and Elizabeth won guest spots on a popular daytime soap opera. *One thing's for sure, I'm going to have to pull off the performance of a lifetime with Jeremy on Friday night. . . .*

The phone rang and she jumped nervously. Elizabeth answered it in her room; Jessica heard her sister shout through the connecting bathroom. "Jess, it's for you."

Her heart in her throat, Jessica reached for the phone. "H-hello?"

"Jessica, it's Ken. How're you doing?"

Limp with relief, Jessica collapsed back onto the bed; she'd been expecting Jeremy's voice. "Oh, pretty good," she breathed. "Kind of not in the mood for homework, but if I don't crack my science book soon, I'll fail Russo's quiz tomorrow."

"Tell me about it," Ken commiserated. "I've stalled out on my French assignment—Ms. Dalton must've been possessed. She gave us about a million irregular verbs to conjugate."

Jessica laughed. "She does get carried away sometimes."

"Well, anyway . . ." Jessica waited for Ken to tell her the real reason he'd called; she knew it wasn't to talk about homework. "So I was just wondering," he said, his tone casual, "if you were planning on going to the Mistletoe Madness dance on Friday. Actually, what I was *really* wondering is if you'd like to go with me."

"Oh, that's right. The dance." She was about to say sure, she'd love to, when she remembered what was going to happen on Friday night. "I'm sorry, Ken, I wish I could, but . . . I've got other plans."

If Ken wondered whether her other plans involved Jeremy, he was too polite to ask. "That's OK, Jess. Hey, I'll see you around."

"You bet," she said with false cheer. "Thanks for calling."

"Take it easy."

She hung up the phone, her lips pouting with disappointment. Ken's invitation seemed out of the blue . . . or was it? Their paths seemed to be crossing a lot lately. *Ken Matthews and me . . . hmm,* she

159

speculated, her complexion washing over with a warm, pink glow. The star quarterback and the head cheerleader, two gorgeous blondes . . . it had occurred to Jessica in the past that they'd make a dynamite couple. Now the more she thought about it, the more she wished she could go with him to the dance.

I suppose Ken will just ask someone else, Jessica thought with a sigh. As worried as she was about how things were going to end with Jeremy, her natural effervescent optimism managed to bubble to the surface. *Oh, well. After this weekend I can start living a normal life again. I'll put this horrible episode with Jeremy behind me, and maybe I'll miss the dance, but that doesn't mean I can't take advantage of the mistletoe!*

The Mistletoe Madness decorations committee had been hard at work after school on Thursday, so that by Friday the halls and gymnasium of Sweet Valley High had been transformed into a winter wonderland. Walls and ceilings were draped with red-and-white streamers and flocked pine garlands; the lobby was accented with balloon bouquets and cutouts of Santa, elves, and reindeer; the majority of students and teachers had dressed in colors of red, green, and white.

Todd, wearing white jeans and a spruce-green polo shirt, met Elizabeth at her locker before the first bell. "Looks like you forgot what day it is," he observed.

160

Elizabeth glanced down at her short denim skirt and purple mock turtleneck. "I did," she admitted. "I guess I've just been thinking about . . . other things."

"Like what?"

Elizabeth half turned away from him on the pretense of sorting through the books in her locker. "Well, something's come up," she said at last. "I know you're going to be disappointed, Todd, but . . . I can't go to the dance with you tonight after all."

Todd leaned against the adjacent locker so he could peer into her face. "Liz, you sound—what's going on? Is this something to do with Sue and Jeremy?"

Elizabeth nodded. "Come on," she said, slamming her locker. "Let's find someplace where we can talk privately."

A minute later they were sequestered in an out-of-the-way stairwell. Elizabeth recapped recent developments in the Sue-Jeremy-Jessica melodrama for Todd. When she was finished, he whistled. "Unbelievable," he declared. "So the whole time Sue thought she and Jeremy were just using Jessica, Jeremy was actually using her, too, and now he's found a way to hijack her inheritance!"

"Nice guy, huh?"

"It sounds like you have enough to go to the police," said Todd.

"We're almost there, but not quite. Our plan is

to call Sam Diamond this afternoon and see if she can drive up from L.A. to help us out. Of course, it all hinges on Jessica's phone call to Jeremy. . . ."

Elizabeth sketched the details for Todd. He frowned. "I don't know, Liz," he said gruffly. "It sounds pretty dangerous to me."

"Sam's a professional," she reminded him. "She can get backup if we need it."

He shook his head. "I still don't like it. The four of you walking straight into the lion's den . . ." A light flickered in his dark eyes. "I'm going with you."

"You really don't need to. We'll be fine—"

"There's safety in numbers. I'm going with you," he insisted.

Finally Elizabeth nodded her assent. As Todd wrapped his strong arms around her, she relaxed— she felt safer, less on edge, already. No doubt about it, it would be great to have Todd along for moral support if nothing else. But of course it was Jessica who was really running the biggest risk. Jessica would be alone with Jeremy. . . .

"Maybe this isn't a good idea after all," Elizabeth said to Jessica after school. "We haven't told Mom and Dad what's going on, and we haven't gone back to the police with this new evidence against Jeremy, and sure, Sam carries a gun, but what if—"

Jessica held up a hand. "We've almost got this

guy, but one wrong move on our part and he'll be out of here. They'd never catch him, and Sue would never see a penny of her inheritance."

Elizabeth was still twisting a strand of her hair anxiously. "What if he doesn't take the bait, though?"

"I think he'll take it." Jessica's expression was grim. "If I know Jeremy Randall at all . . ."

For a long moment the two sisters gazed deep into each other's eyes, taking silent strength from each other. Then Jessica gestured toward the door. "OK, Liz. I think I need privacy for this."

"Good luck," Elizabeth whispered before disappearing into her own room.

Jessica paced her bedroom, trying to compose herself. Stopping in front of the window, she stared outside. It was a gray, windy day; fallen leaves danced in crazy circles on the lawn, and a few fat drops of rain spattered against the windowpanes. *There's a storm building,* Jessica thought, pressing her hands against her stomach to calm her own internal whirlwind. *It's going to be a wild night. . . .*

Turning on her heel, she walked purposefully over to her nightstand. She drew a few deep breaths, then picked up the telephone.

It rang four times on the other end; Jessica was about to hang up when someone finally answered. "Hello?" said Jeremy.

"Jeremy, it's Jessica," she said calmly.

"Jess! I thought you'd dropped off the face of the globe."

"No, I'm still here. And I have something to tell you."

His tone was teasing. "About why you've been too busy to see me?"

"Not exactly." She drew another deep breath. "Jeremy, I know all about you."

There was a moment of tense silence. Then Jeremy asked carefully, "What exactly do you mean?"

"I know about you and Sue," Jessica told him, twisting the phone cord around her hand to keep it from shaking, "that you two are still romantically involved, and that the whole thing between you and me was just part of a scam to get the inheritance back from my mother. And I know that you figured out a way to steal Sue's money from the account in New York."

She could hear Jeremy breathing heavily. "How did you find out all this?" he asked, his voice hoarse.

"It doesn't matter how I found out, I just—"

"What are you going to do? Are you going to turn me in? Because if you do—"

"Wait, Jeremy, just listen to me," Jessica begged, trying hard for just the right element of vulnerability. "I know everything, but it doesn't matter to me. I forgive you—I still love you. We really did have something, you know we did, and I

164

know that's why you decided to ditch Sue instead of spending your life with her. It's true, isn't it, Jeremy? You do care about me, at least a little—it wasn't all an act?"

"I . . . I want to know where you're planning to go with all this," said Jeremy. There was an edge to his voice; she hadn't quite convinced him yet.

Jessica pulled out all the stops. "I want to be with you, Jeremy, that's all I want—all I've ever wanted. I'm sick of my family trying to keep us apart, and everybody trying to tell me I'm too young to know my own heart. I'm glad you've done this to Sue—I hate her, I really hate her. I'd do anything to get back at her—I just wish I could see her face when she finds out she's lost you *and* the money. Take me with you, Jeremy," she pleaded, her voice husky with desire and abandon. "Let's run away together."

"So you'd give it all up—your family, your life here—you'd give it all up to be with me, even though you know I'm no Prince Charming," he said with a smug, cynical laugh.

Jessica fought back her disgust and outrage. *What a creepy, egotistical, sick, twisted . . .*

The hardest part about this moment was that a measure of her disgust was aimed at herself. Jeremy's response made Jessica see how foolishly, spinelessly lovesick she had been before, that Jeremy would think this behavior was in character. "I love you, Jeremy," she said, nearly choking on the words that used to flow so easily, so innocently, from her lips. "I want to be with you. Nothing and no one else matters to me nearly as much—it's that simple."

"Well, I'd kind of got used to the idea of enjoying all this money by myself," Jeremy admitted with a laugh, "but maybe it wouldn't be so bad sharing my tropical paradise with you."

"I'm ready now," Jessica told him. "I could meet you tonight."

"You'll have to, because I'm leaving the country in the morning." Suddenly his tone was rough, menacing. "You swear you haven't told anyone else about this?"

"Not a soul. It's just you and me, Jeremy. By the time they figure out we've taken off together, we'll be long gone."

"Long gone . . ." He savored the words, as if he had a private joke he wasn't sharing. "OK, Jessica Wakefield. I want you as much as you want me." His voice vibrated with passion. "I'll pick you up at eight tonight, and we'll go to the Project Nature cabin. Don't tell anyone where you're going or who you're meeting, and don't leave any good-bye notes. We can't leave a trail."

"You can count on me," she promised. "I can't wait to be with you, Jeremy."

She could almost see his evil smile. "Get ready for the ride of your life, baby."

When the phone call was over, Jessica realized

that her entire body was trembling, just like the saplings outside buffeted by the rising wind.

Jeremy had bought her story, hook, line, and sinker. She'd set the wheel in motion. Tonight was the night.

Later that afternoon Jessica looked up from the TV in the family room to see her mother standing in the hall. "Hi, Mom. What are you doing home from work so early?"

Mrs. Wakefield stepped into the family room and dropped her briefcase and linen blazer onto a chair with an exaggerated sigh. "I had one of those meetings after lunch," she said, grimacing. "The kind where everyone's talking at once and no one will listen to anyone else's point of view and you just want to . . ." She gestured with both hands, pretending to strangle someone.

Jessica laughed. "But, Mom, I thought you had infinite patience!"

Alice smiled wryly. "You've put me to the test often enough, that's for sure."

Jessica fought back the urge to tell her mother about Jeremy's treachery, to assure her that the relationship was over, that Mr. and Mrs. Wakefield didn't have to worry and disapprove anymore. Instead, she said, "I'm not such a horrible kid, am I?"

"Of course not, honey." Crossing the room, Mrs. Wakefield planted a kiss on Jessica's cheek.

"You have a mind of your own, but that's not a bad thing."

Fumbling on the sofa for the remote, Jessica flicked off the television. "I don't know why I waste my time watching these dumb soaps," she said.

"Because you're a hopeless romantic." Mrs. Wakefield sat down next to her daughter. "Like me."

Jessica wrinkled her nose, laughing. *"You're* a romantic? No way, Mom. You're always the voice of reason and restraint!"

"Maybe as a parent, but not necessarily as a person," Mrs. Wakefield said. "I can be pretty impetuous."

Jessica looked at her doubtfully. "I guess you *were* pretty wild when you were young, like the time you broke off your wedding to Hank Patman at the last minute so you could be with Dad."

"Actually, that wasn't impetuous at all," her mother said. "That was the most carefully thought-through, heart-sure decision I ever made. I've never regretted it for an instant."

Jessica sighed heavily. *"I've never regretted it for an instant"—sure can't say that about my romance with Jeremy!* "Mom," she said, leaning her head against Mrs. Wakefield's shoulder. "How did you know about Dad? I mean, how did you know he was the one?"

"Well, from the first we felt an incredibly strong connection—you know, a mutual attraction."

"So it was like . . ." Jessica was embarrassed to

say the word in reference to her parents. "Passion?"

"Definitely passion." Mrs. Wakefield tickled Jessica's rib. "But that was just one part of it, and ultimately not the most important part."

"What was the most important part, then?"

Mrs. Wakefield considered for a moment. "I'd say trust was, and is, the most important element of an enduring relationship."

"And you had that with Dad, from the start?"

"From the start," her mother confirmed. "The very first day we met, your father saved me from drowning at the beach. He didn't know me at all, but he saved my life, and when I looked into his eyes, I saw something honest and deep and real. It was an unspoken promise to always be there when I needed him, to never let me down."

"Wow. And has he always been there for you?"

"Always, and our trust in each other just grows deeper with every passing year."

Jessica pondered this for a moment in chastened silence. "So I guess passion without trust isn't worth a whole lot, huh?" she asked at last in a small voice.

"It's not that it's not worth something," replied Mrs. Wakefield, "but I don't think you can count on it lasting very long."

Talk about the understatement of the century, thought Jessica sadly.

Mrs. Wakefield twisted on the couch so she

could face her daughter. "I want you to know something about yourself, Jess," she said, her blue-green eyes serious. "You're a very special person, and a strong person. You deserve the best, and that's why I expect so much from you. Do you understand that?"

Jessica nodded, her own eyes suddenly sparkling with tears.

Mrs. Wakefield gently stroked her daughter's hair. "We haven't talked like this in a long time. Things have been kind of rocky in this household, and your father and I were pretty critical of some of your behavior, but that doesn't mean either he or I have stopped loving you for a single second. You mean the world to me."

Mrs. Wakefield wrapped her arms around Jessica, and Jessica hugged her back with all her might. *Mom believes in me,* Jessica thought, infused with a new courage and confidence. *Maybe I always knew that, deep down inside—maybe that's why I'm going to have the strength to stand up to Jeremy tonight. . . .*

"Maybe it wasn't such a great idea to wait until the last minute to phone Sam Diamond," said Sue, glancing nervously at the clock over the mantel in the Wakefields' living room. "It's already seven o'clock. What if she doesn't get here in time?"

"We had to wait," Elizabeth reasoned. "We had to make sure Sam wouldn't have a chance to tell

Mom and Dad. If they knew what we were up to, they wouldn't have gone out to dinner—they would have stayed home to keep an eye on us. There's no way they'd let Jessica go out with Jeremy tonight if they'd heard the whole story."

"Maybe Jessica *shouldn't* go out with Jeremy tonight." Sue's face was pale, and dark shadows circled her eyes; Elizabeth guessed she hadn't gotten a good night's sleep in weeks. "What if he was only pretending to believe her, and he's just luring her to the cabin so he can . . ."

She couldn't finish her sentence. Elizabeth turned to Jessica, a coil of fear tightening in her gut. "He believed me," Jessica assured her dryly. "The guy's ego is so out of control, he'd believe anything. And he's used to thinking of you and me as totally devoted rag dolls he can manipulate any way he likes," she reminded Sue. "Don't worry, he doesn't suspect a thing. He and I will get to the cabin, and I'll get a full confession out of him, which will be on tape because I'll be wired, and then Sam will jump in, and how do they say it in the movies?" She smiled. "The jig will be up."

Todd put an arm around Elizabeth's shoulder, and she leaned against him gratefully, wishing she could feel as confident as Jessica sounded. "I hope it happens that way," she said.

Sue had been sitting on the couch by the window. Now she jumped up, pointing to the headlights beaming into the driveway. "Here she is!"

171

The four rushed to the door to greet Sam. The detective blew into the front hallway along with a gust of chilly, rain-edged wind. "It's really getting ugly out there!" she declared, smoothing her sleek, wheat-blond hair with one gloved hand.

Slipping out of her Burberry raincoat, Sam tossed it across the banister. As usual, the private eye was wearing heels and a stylish, feminine suit; her makeup and accessories were perfect. The expression in her eyes, however, was tough and businesslike. "We don't have much time," Sam said, ushering Todd and the girls toward the kitchen. "Let's sit down—I'd like to show you what I've got on Jeremy and go over our plan for tonight one more time."

They all pulled up chairs around the kitchen table, and Sam removed a fat manila file from her briefcase. "I'd just reached the same conclusion you all did," she began, opening the folder. "In fact, I was getting ready to head to the Sweet Valley police station when Elizabeth called me this afternoon. From the start I was curious about Jeremy, and the fact that computer records revealed absolutely nothing about his past struck me as suspicious rather than not."

"That's how I felt when I did some research on INFOMAX," Elizabeth agreed.

"I did some voice analysis," Sam went on, "comparing the taped messages played by the kidnapper to my taped interview with Jeremy. The results were intriguing, but inconclusive. There was a possible match between the two, but the evidence wasn't clear-cut enough to warrant an arrest. Then I found this."

Thumbing through her papers, she located a photocopy of a microfilmed newspaper article. She handed the photocopy to Sue.

Elizabeth read eagerly over Sue's shoulder. The three-year-old article, from a midwestern paper, recounted how a young man named John Ryder stole a small fortune from his new bride, Kerry LaSalle. The man was never apprehended, the money never recovered. Elizabeth stared at the photo. "John Ryder is Jeremy Randall!" she cried.

Sue dropped the article and pressed both hands to her face. "He's a monster, roaming all over the country preying on stupid rich girls like me and Marla Tannenbaum and this Kerry LaSalle. I just can't believe it—I can't believe I was so naive."

Sam directed a steady gaze at Sue. "Jeremy had to go to special lengths to get his hands on your money," she observed, her tone firm but compassionate. "You were his accomplice in some of his wrongdoing, and that's not something you can go back and undo at this point."

"I know." Sue hung her head. "But now . . . all I want now is to make amends. I don't care about the money, but I don't want him to have it. I don't want him to go on hurting people."

"I guess we all know what we have to do." Sam

clasped her hands on the table. "Jessica, are you ready for this?"

Jessica nodded. "I have a little suitcase packed so it will look like I really *am* prepared to run off with Jeremy. When he picks me up, you guys will be hiding in Sam's car in the garage—you'll give us a head start and then follow us to the cabin."

"We won't let you out of our sight," Sam promised. "You'll be wired, and we'll be in the car listening and recording every incriminating word Jeremy says. As soon as we get what we need, we'll come in after you. The police will be right on our heels."

Jessica straightened her shoulders and flashed a brave smile. "OK, then. Let's do it!"

A quarter of an hour later Jessica stood in the living room with her suitcase and a yellow rain slicker. A small microphone was pinned to her bra, and a power pack was attached to her belt, underneath her sweater. Before following Sam, Todd, and Sue into the garage, Elizabeth gave her sister a quick embrace. "I think you're incredibly brave, Jess," she whispered. "Be careful, OK?"

Jessica returned the hug. "You guys are going to be right there with me. I'm not scared."

With both Mr. Wakefield's cars gone, Sam had been able to back her car into the garage next to the Jeep. With the garage door open but the lights out, the car was in shadow while maintaining a clear view of the driveway and street.

Sam, Elizabeth, Sue, and Todd sat crouched in

the dark car, their eyes fixed on the street. The rain was really lashing down now; when the headlights finally appeared, they were murky and muted.

Elizabeth tensed in the passenger seat. "It's him," she whispered.

Todd reached forward from the back to squeeze her shoulder. Sam had her hand on the key in the ignition, ready to start the engine at any moment.

The car stopped on the street rather than pulling into the driveway. The horn sounded once, twice. Elizabeth gnawed on her knuckles, sick with anxiety. Had Jessica chickened out? Where was she?

Then they saw a slim figure in a yellow jacket dash out into the rainy night, the decoy suitcase in her hand. "There she goes," murmured Todd.

Elizabeth gulped. It was too late for Jessica or any of them to back out. *Be careful, Jess,* she prayed silently. Even though she knew they would stay right behind Jeremy and Jessica, Elizabeth couldn't help being afraid for her sister. Deathly afraid.

Chapter 12

They'd left Sweet Valley far behind. Jeremy was driving fast on the back country roads—too fast, Jessica thought, trying not to jump out of her skin every time they skidded around a bend in the road, tires squealing. Bad weather made the driving even more treacherous. The rain was still slanting down and the roads were slick.

Jeremy had popped a tape into the cassette player, and the volume was turned up loud; Jessica was thankful that she didn't have to make small talk. On the pretense of checking her makeup, she tipped the visor so she could see behind her with the mirror. A pair of headlights was dimly visible through the curtain of rain. *They're still there*, she thought, relaxing somewhat.

She flipped up the visor and leaned back in her seat. Holding the steering wheel with one hand, Jeremy slid his arm across the top of her seat and massaged her shoulder. "You feel tense," he observed.

"Oh, I . . ." Jessica raised her voice to be heard over the music. "I guess I'm a little keyed up, you know? I mean, this is a pretty big step. I've left home, and I'm never going back." She laughed almost hysterically. "That's not the kind of thing a person does every day."

"You won't regret it." He flashed her a smile that was wide but ice-cold. Jessica shivered. "We're going to have a real good time."

Ahead there was a fork in the road. Gunning the engine, Jeremy careened to the right. Another quarter mile down, he swung right again onto a poorly marked crossroad. The road continued to climb, zigzagging ever higher. Looking out the window, Jessica saw that the rain had turned to sleet. Turning casually in her seat as if to look at Jeremy, she glanced over her shoulder. Instead of the reassuring headlights, her eyes met nothing but blackness.

She continued to stare behind her, holding her breath and praying. *They've got to be back there, they're just hidden by a curve in the road, by the trees. . . .*

But no. Apparently, Sam and the others were no longer trailing Jeremy's car. They had been left behind by his speed and the stormy night.

Jessica faced forward again, her breath coming

in short, painful gasps. *They know the way,* she reminded herself. *Maybe they're lagging, but they'll get there. It'll be OK.*

The sleet changed to snow. A storybook landscape raced along outside the car: pine trees decked with capes of white fluffy flakes, glowing softly in the snow-filled night. Jeremy slowed the car only slightly to compensate for the lack of traction. "We're almost there," he told Jessica, his voice ebullient.

They passed a number of driveways leading to A-frame mountain cabins. Then, for a mile or so, there was nothing but forest. Jessica remembered the last time she'd been to the Project Nature cabin, on Halloween night. It was completely isolated, with no other house for miles around. . . .

Soon they were bumping down an unpaved driveway covered with snow. Ahead of them, through the trees, Jessica glimpsed the cabin. It was dark under its new mantle of snow, creepy and deserted.

I can't go in there with him, Jessica thought desperately. *I know—when he gets out of the car, I'll slide over to the driver's seat and take off. I'll leave him here and just go home. I don't care if he escapes with all of Sue's money, I can't go in there with him.*

Jeremy tapped the brakes, and the car rolled to a stop. He killed the engine and the headlights. For a moment they sat in the dark car, listening to the whispering of the wind and snow in the pines.

As he opened the door on his side of the car, Jeremy removed the key from the ignition and slid them into the front pocket of his jeans. Jessica gulped down her fear. So much for that route of escape. *You can't run away now, anyhow,* she told herself. *You have a job to do.* And of course, if she thought about it for a few seconds, it made sense for Sam to hang back, just out of sight. They didn't want Jeremy to catch on to the fact that he was being followed.

Jeremy walked around to the passenger side and opened the door for her. She stepped out, taking a deep breath of the cold, sharp mountain air.

"Here we are," Jeremy said, his voice heavy with meaning. "Alone at last."

Jessica blinked at him, flakes of snow catching on her long eyelashes.

Placing a firm hand against the small of her back, Jeremy propelled her toward the cabin. "It's not exactly the romantic love nest by the ocean that we were thinking of," he went on, "but it'll do, eh, Jessica?"

Jessica nodded weakly. Naturally, Jeremy assumed she still wanted to sleep with him, since supposedly she loved him enough to run away with him. *That's why he brought me here,* she thought, her heart in her throat. *It's not just so we can hide out. He has something else in mind. . . .*

❖   ❖   ❖

179

"I don't remember this road," Elizabeth said, peering out the car window and biting her lip. "That rocky hill, and the stream . . ." She shook her head. "No, this isn't the road that leads to the Project Nature cabin."

The car was lurching from side to side on the uneven pavement; Sam gripped the wheel tightly, leaning forward so she could see through the snow-splattered windshield. Even on high speed, the wipers didn't have much effect against the fast-flying snow.

"We must have taken a wrong turn," Todd surmised. "Back at that fork in the road."

Sam was cursing softly under her breath. "OK, we'll go back. The road widens a bit up ahead—I'll make a U-turn."

She lifted her foot from the gas pedal and downshifted, then tapped the brakes cautiously. Suddenly the car was spinning on the icy road like an amusement-park ride.

Elizabeth was flung hard against the dashboard. Sue screamed shrilly, "Oh, my God, we're going to crash!"

The car skidded in a full circle and kept going. All four passengers bounced wildly as the car bucked over the side of the road and jolted to a stop in a ditch.

The engine died. For a shocked moment Elizabeth, Todd, Sam, and Sue were still and quiet; then they all started speaking at once. "Are you all right up there?" Todd called.

"Anybody hurt?" asked Sam.

Elizabeth tipped her head from side to side experimentally. Her neck felt a little wrenched, but other than that she was fine. "We're OK," Sue reported from the backseat.

"Thank God for seat belts," exclaimed Sam, unbuckling hers. "Come on, guys. We've got to get out of this ditch. We don't have any time to waste!"

Shoving open their doors, they jumped out into the snow. "You got your U-turn, Sam," Todd pointed out wryly. "We went around one and a half rotations—we're pointed back the way we came!"

Sam bent to examine the tires. "We didn't get a flat—that's one stroke of luck."

"But it's going to take some pushing," Elizabeth predicted. "Underneath the snow, the ground is pretty muddy."

"Let's take a crack at it," said Todd, striding to the back of the car.

Sam slid back in behind the wheel. Fortunately, the engine started again on the first try. Elizabeth and Sue took up positions on either side of Todd, bracing themselves. "One, two, three," Todd counted. "Push!"

Sam stepped on the gas. With all their might, Elizabeth, Todd, and Sue pushed against the car. The tires spun uselessly, kicking up a shower of snow and mud. "It's not working!" Sue cried.

Sam let up on the gas. Todd stepped back, wiping his hands on his jacket. "We're not going to make it," Sue sobbed. "Oh, why did we ever even try this? He'll kill her! He wasn't going to share the money with me—why would he share it with her? He'll kill her, and it will be all my—"

"Sue!" Grabbing Sue's shoulders, Elizabeth shook her hard. "We don't have time for this. We've got to put this car back on the road if we die trying!"

Die trying, die trying . . . The words circled like blizzard-tossed snowflakes in Elizabeth's brain as she leaned against the trunk of Sam's car, pushing with all her desperate strength. She wouldn't allow herself to think about what might happen to her sister if they didn't find their way to the Project Nature cabin . . . and soon.

Jeremy had started a fire in the fireplace and lit a few candles, but for Jessica the mood and setting were anything but romantic. She sat stiffly on the sofa, her eyes trained warily on Jeremy, who was making calls from the cellular phone.

He stood on the opposite side of the room, his back to Jessica. She could hear only snatches of the conversation. "You moved the money . . . a new account? Under what name? Immediate access . . ."

Nibbling her nails, Jessica glanced around the room. The cabin was decorated for the holidays—there was a Christmas tree glittering with lights and ornaments, pine garlands along the mantel, and paper-cutout snowflakes on the windows.

There must be another Project Nature party coming up, Jessica surmised. *If only someone would show up tonight. . . .*

But she knew that was highly improbable. Who but a madman would be out on the roads on a night like this?

A madman . . . Jessica stared at Jeremy, her mouth dry as cotton. No, he was cold and calculating, greedy, cruel, and immoral, but he wasn't a madman. He might go by any number of aliases—Jeremy Randall, Matt Thorn, John Ryder—but he knew exactly who he was, and exactly what he was doing, at every minute of the day.

After scribbling some notes on a pad of paper on the end table, Jeremy turned off the cellular phone. "Is—is everything going the way it's supposed to?" Jessica asked, hoping she sounded like a nervous but trusting girlfriend.

"You bet." Jeremy faced Jessica, his dark eyes flashing with some unreadable emotion. "With me everything always goes the way it's supposed to."

Jessica cast a sideways, flirtatious glance at him. "Oh, is that so?"

Her teasing, provoking manner had the desired effect. Jeremy's mood grew expansive; he was ready to boast about his exploits. "You know it is. You figured me out. Hey, how did you find out about all this, anyway?"

Jessica shook a finger at him playfully. "Maybe

I'm throwing aside everything to be with you, but I get to keep some secrets, don't I?"

He crossed the room to stand in front of her, a leering smile on his face. "I'm all for keeping a few secrets. As long as this isn't a story you spread around town."

"No one else knows," Jessica swore, checking her impulse to glance toward the window. *Sam, Liz, Todd, and Sue must be here by now,* she thought, listening to the wind and snow sighing outside. *I'll get Jeremy to admit a few more things, and then Sam will have enough to go on and they can burst in and rescue me.*

"I really can't believe you were just stringing me along, though," Jessica continued, pretending to pout. "You *do* love me, don't you, Jeremy? It wasn't all an act?"

"Sure, I love you," he said carelessly. Dropping next to her on the couch, he slung a possessive arm around her shoulders. "But at first, I've got to admit, I just had my sights set on Sue's half million."

She forced herself to snuggle close to him. "But you'd rather have me and the money instead of the money all by itself, wouldn't you?"

"Oh, yeah. Of course."

"This wasn't the first time you pulled a scam like this, was it?" she asked, looking up at him with wide, innocently curious eyes.

"Naw, Sue wasn't the first. There've been a

couple—a girl in Atlanta, and one in Grosse Pointe, Michigan. Let me tell you, having money doesn't make a person smart. A little sweet talk, and those girls were putty in my hands."

A little sweet talk . . . It made Jessica sick to remember how fast *she'd* fallen for Jeremy's sweet talk. "So when you met Sue and found out her mother was about to die and make her rich, you decided she'd be your next victim."

He nodded, puffing out his chest a little. "We were engaged within a month. It was going to be the easiest money I ever made, but then Mrs. Gibbons changed her will, and the whole deal just got more and more complicated."

"But if it hadn't, you wouldn't have met me," Jessica pointed out.

He smiled down at her, a coldly amused light in his eyes. "That's right, darlin'. Speaking of which . . ."

Lowering his face to hers, he kissed her long and hard on the mouth. His behavior was rougher, more callous—clearly he felt she was in his power and he could do whatever he liked with her.

She tried her hardest to fake some enthusiasm, and Jeremy didn't seem to suspect anything. A moment later he drew back from her. "You stay right here and make yourself comfortable," he said huskily, placing heavy hands on her shoulders. "I'll be right back, and then . . ."

Jeremy disappeared in the direction of the

downstairs bathroom. As soon as he was out of sight, Jessica leaped to her feet. Dashing to the window, she pushed the curtain aside and peered out into the snowy night.

Where are they? she wondered, panic slicing into her heart like a knife. Sam's car was nowhere in sight; as far as she could see, the snow lay in a deep, soft blanket, undisturbed by footprints.

Jessica raced to the other side of the cabin. The same view met her eyes from that window. *Oh, no! They didn't make it.* The realization hit her like an avalanche. The whole time she'd been sitting on the couch with Jeremy, pressing him about his criminal past, Jessica had felt protected by her knowledge that help was just a shout away. *I'm alone here,* Jessica thought, her teeth suddenly chattering. *They got lost or had an accident. I'm alone.*

When Jeremy returned, he was going to expect something from her, and Jessica had a feeling he wasn't about to take no for an answer.

For a split second she considered running out into the snowy night. But how far would she get in this storm? Jeremy would immediately suspect the worst—he'd go after her, and then who knows what he'd do to her.

Her desperate eyes raked the room and settled on the cellular phone. *I'll call the police,* Jessica decided, inspired. She hoped Sam had already called them . . . she hoped they were on their way. . . .

She knew she had to act fast. As she picked up the phone, she noticed the paper Jeremy had been writing on. She picked that up, too, squinting at the numbers scrawled there. "A bank-account number," she whispered. "This is where Sue's money is!"

It was the best piece of evidence they were going to get. Jessica was still holding the paper, rapidly trying to memorize the number, when Jeremy suddenly reappeared. "What are you doing?" he roared.

Jessica gasped, dropping both the phone and the scrap of paper.

"I—nothing, I was just—"

His handsome face twisted, contorted with fury into a hideous mask. "I knew I couldn't trust you!" he snarled, springing at her with his hands outstretched. "You've made a big mistake, Jessica Wakefield, a big mistake!"

Jessica backed away from Jeremy, her eyes wide with terror. "I wasn't doing anything," she squeaked. "I was just . . . I was going to call my parents and let them know I'm OK. I didn't leave a note because you told me not to, but I don't want them to worry—"

Jeremy stalked her purposefully. "The paper. What were you doing with the paper?" he barked.

"I just . . . picked it up. I don't know what it means, and I don't care. Jeremy, I—"

"You were planning to turn me in, weren't

you?" he guessed. "You stupid, stupid girl. . . ."

He leaped toward her. Screaming, Jessica raced for the door. Jeremy overtook her; his hands fumbled at her throat. Twisting, she kicked his kneecap, then whirled from his grasp. She clawed desperately at the door handle, but he was on her again, panting and cursing.

"No, Jeremy," Jessica cried as he gripped her shoulders and tried to wrestle her to the ground. "The police are coming and Sam Diamond—it's not worth it. You'll only—"

Mustering every last, desperate ounce of strength, Jessica managed to wrench herself free. Thrown off balance, Jeremy careened against the Christmas tree. It started to topple. As she dodged sideways to avoid being struck, Jessica caught her toe under the edge of the rug. Suddenly, she was sailing through the air. The last thing she saw before losing consciousness was the hard corner of the wooden coffee table rising up to meet her.

The tinsel-covered Christmas tree had fallen across the end table where Jeremy had set a couple of flickering candles. With a crackling roar the flames crawled around the tree, devouring the tinsel and other garlands.

On the other side of the room, his arms hanging limply at his sides, Jeremy stood breathing heavily. He gazed down at Jessica's unconscious body, his eyes devoid of emotion.

"Better it happens this way," he muttered to himself. He'd never intended to take Jessica with him to the South Pacific, to share Sue's fortune with her. He'd just gone along with her proposal to keep her quiet . . . and to lure her to the cabin so he could get rid of her before she blew his cover.

The Christmas tree was burning brightly; the flames licked along the walls, moving around the cabin closer and closer to Jessica's prone figure. Yes, this was better. *I've managed to avoid murder so far,* Jeremy thought, pleased with himself for being such a purist. Jessica's death would look like an accident, and he wouldn't have to dirty his hands by actually killing her.

The room was filling with smoke. Jeremy blew a kiss in Jessica's direction. "Good night, sweetheart," he called as he hurried toward the door. "Sorry we never had that romantic rendezvous."

Flinging the door open, Jeremy dashed out into the snow, leaving Jessica behind to die in the fire.

189

Chapter 13

"This is it!" Sue cried, leaning forward in her seat and pointing. "The road to the cabin!"

Hauling on the wheel, Sam steered the car onto the bumpy, unplowed road. She was driving faster now, throwing caution to the wind as they neared their destination.

"Around the next bend," said Elizabeth. Her hand already on the door handle, she was ready to leap out as soon as the car slowed near the cabin. "Just past that group of pine trees. . . ."

They jolted around a curve, the tires skidding slightly on the snow. Ahead of them, the Project Nature cabin stood in a clearing, its first-floor windows glowing with a strong light. Elizabeth stared at the flickering orange glimmer. *Too bright for electric lights.* . . . "It's on fire!" she screamed. "Jessica!"

Sam slammed on the brakes. At that moment the engine of a car parked just a few yards away roared to life. "It's Jeremy," exclaimed Todd, jumping from Sam's car. "He's getting away!"

Todd waved his arms, trying to block the car's path, but with a hard yank on the steering wheel, Jeremy sped around him. "He's alone!" Elizabeth shouted, beckoning to Todd to follow her. "We can't go after him now. Jessica must still be in the cabin. We have to get her out!"

The four ran through the falling snow toward the cabin. As they drew closer, they could see flames pulsing against the downstairs windows. Jeremy hadn't closed the door behind him, and now a draft of air blew it all the way open, giving them a glimpse of the raging furnace within.

As they neared the door, Sam halted, raising a hand to shield her face from the warmth of the blaze. "It's too late!" she cried. "The fire's out of control—we can't go in there!"

Deaf to Sam's warning, Elizabeth continued forward, her steps as deliberate as a robot's. She was oblivious to the danger; she could think of only one thing. *My twin sister is in there, and she'll die if I don't go in after her. Without her I wouldn't want to go on living. . . .*

Elizabeth reached the door. "No, Liz!" Todd shouted.

Elizabeth stepped into the inferno.

The heat was searing, and choking smoke filled

191

the air. Coughing, Elizabeth pushed forward, tripping over burning debris. Suddenly she heard a loud crack like a gunshot. Looking up, she saw a burning beam about to fall from the ceiling.

She might have remained standing there, paralyzed with fear, and been crushed and burned, but someone shoved her to the side. When the beam fell with a resounding crash, it missed her by a couple of feet. Elizabeth wasn't alone. "Sue!" she gasped, clutching the other girl's arm.

Sue gestured with one hand, covering her mouth and nose with the other. "Over there!" she yelled. "I think I see her!"

Crouching, they made their way toward the center of the room. A girl was lying on the floor; as they drew near, she raised herself on one elbow and started to cough. "Jessica!" Elizabeth cried.

"Come on, we don't have a second to waste!" Sue urged.

Together, Elizabeth and Sue helped Jessica to her feet and dragged her as quickly as they could manage to the door. As the three stumbled outside, they heard a sound like a thousand agonized screams. Just a moment after Todd and Sam pulled them to safety, the second floor of the Project Nature cabin collapsed into the first in an explosion of smoke and sparks.

The five stood in a puddle of melting snow, watching the conflagration. Jessica leaned weakly against Elizabeth and Todd, coughing and crying.

Elizabeth hugged her sister close, her face pressed against Jessica's singed hair. Over the top of Jessica's head, Elizabeth met Sue's gaze. Brimming with tears of gratitude, Elizabeth's eyes spoke to Sue without a need for words. *Thank you for saving my sister's life.*

"Start at the beginning," Ned Wakefield urged Elizabeth.

After receiving an urgent phone call from their daughter, Mr. and Mrs. Wakefield had met Elizabeth and the others at the hospital where Jessica was being treated for bruises and smoke inhalation. Now Elizabeth, her parents, and Todd were sitting in the visitors' lounge with a pot of coffee on the table between them. Sam and Sue talked in low, serious tones on the other side of the room.

Elizabeth took a deep breath. "It was all a plot to get Sue's inheritance back," she said, "and Sue was in on it with Jeremy at first. Then, just when she decided she didn't want to go along with his crazy, greedy schemes any longer, she discovered he had a secret agenda of his own. He was planning to steal her fortune and then desert her—he never intended to marry Sue *or* Jessica."

By the time Elizabeth finished updating her parents—she ended her taut narrative with an account of the rescue at the burning cabin—both Mr. and Mrs. Wakefield were pale. "I—I just don't know what to think or feel," Mrs. Wakefield murmured after a speechless minute. She tossed a glance at Sue. "She isn't the girl I thought I knew and loved. But she did recognize her mistakes, and she tried to change the course she was on. . . ."

"I think Sue's been pretty mixed up," said Elizabeth. "What she and Jeremy did to Jessica—and to all of us—was terrible. But in the end Sue put her own life on the line to save Jessica's. Maybe that doesn't make up for everything, but it means something, doesn't it?"

"And Jeremy. Will they ever hunt him down?" wondered Mr. Wakefield.

As the four sank into pensive silence, they heard a snatch of Sue's hushed conversation with Sam Diamond. "I'm ready to confess," Sue murmured, her head bowed in an attitude of repentance, ". . . to face my punishment . . ."

Just then a uniformed state trooper strode into the lounge. "Mr. and Mrs. Wakefield, Ms. Diamond. I'd like to report that we've found Jeremy Randall," he announced.

Elizabeth jumped to her feet. "How? Where?"

"We followed his tire tracks from the cabin," the trooper related, "and about five miles down the highway, the tracks skidded off the icy road. We found Randall trapped in the wrecked car."

"Is he . . . dead?" gasped Elizabeth.

"Injured, but alive." The trooper smiled grimly at Sam. "It won't be too hard to make a case against him—he's admitted to using the names Matt Thorn and John Ryder."

Sam stepped out in the hall to talk with the trooper and another police officer. Sue stood by herself, her eyes on the floor, until Mrs. Wakefield spoke to her. "Come here, Sue," she requested, her voice weary but kind.

Sue walked slowly toward Mr. and Mrs. Wakefield, Elizabeth, and Todd. When Mrs. Wakefield held out her arms, Sue rushed to her, tears flowing. "Oh, Alice, can you ever forgive me?"

Mrs. Wakefield stroked Sue's hair, her own eyes shining with tears. "Of course I can," Elizabeth heard her whisper.

Elizabeth tiptoed into the hospital room. There were two beds, separated by a curtain; Jessica was lying on one of them, her eyes closed.

A lump rose in Elizabeth's throat as she gazed down at her sister, whose face and arms were patched with bandages. "We came so close to losing you," she whispered, stretching out a hand to touch Jessica's hair.

Jessica's eyes popped open. "There you are!" she exclaimed, sitting up in bed. "I was wondering when somebody would show up. Can I leave now?"

Elizabeth burst out laughing, her heart flooding with happy relief. "Whoa, take it easy! You just went through a pretty traumatic experience. I think they want to observe you for a little while longer to make sure you're really OK."

"I'm fine," Jessica insisted impatiently. "Just hand me my clothes and—"

She broke off, interrupted by a fit of coughing. Elizabeth eased her sister back onto the pillows. "I guess maybe I did breathe in a lot of smoke," Jessica admitted, gingerly rubbing her raw throat.

Elizabeth sat on the edge of the bed. "You did," she confirmed. "You were . . ." *This close to being burned alive.* Elizabeth closed her eyes for a moment, not wanting to remember the fiery scene at the cabin. "We got to you just in time."

"I can't believe Jeremy was just going to leave me there." Jessica shuddered. "Liz, how could I have been so wrong about him? How could I have been so stupid?"

Elizabeth squeezed her sister's hand. "Face it, Jess," she said with an affectionate smile. "You're not the most logical person under the best of circumstances. And when you're in love . . ."

Jessica laughed wryly. "I don't know if I was ever really in love," she admitted. "I was infatuated, sure. And Jeremy made me feel . . ." She shook her head. "He sure had all the lines and moves down cold. But, then, he'd had lots of practice!"

"You and Sue both learned some hard lessons," Elizabeth commented.

"You can say that again. Poor Sue . . . what do you think will happen to her, Liz?"

Elizabeth shrugged. "I don't know. The fake

kidnapping and ransom-demand thing is a pretty serious offense. But the fact that she's willing to cooperate with the whole investigation . . . I'm sure they'll go easy on her."

"I think she's a good person inside," Jessica said. "Unlike Jeremy." She closed her eyes and sighed. "I still can't believe what a monster he turned out to be. Playing a game with me from the very first minute we 'accidentally' met on the beach . . . I don't think I'll ever be able to trust a guy again."

"Oh, sure you will," Elizabeth assured her, "if he's the right guy."

"But how will I be able to tell he's the right guy?"

"You just have to get to know him a little *before* you fall head over heels crazy in love."

Jessica rolled her eyes, laughing. "Sensible advice from my sensible sister."

"Hey, don't knock it," teased Elizabeth.

Jessica sat up straight again, plumping the pillows behind her back. "All of a sudden I feel a lot better," she declared. "I needed to rest for a few more minutes, that's all. Could you call a nurse for me so I can get checked out of here?"

"What's the rush?" Elizabeth asked.

"Well, speaking of boys, something just occurred to me." Jessica smiled up at Elizabeth, her eyes twinkling merrily. "It's not too late to meet Ken at the Mistletoe Madness dance!"

Here's a sneak preview of Sweet Valley High #112, **Jessica Quits the Squad,** *Book One in a thrilling three-part miniseries. Get ready for cheerleading madness!*

"Great job today, girls!" Ken Matthews said as he walked past the booth of cheerleaders at the Dairi Burger on Friday afternoon. "You guys were hot! We couldn't have won that game without you."

"Thanks," Jessica Wakefield said, gladly accepting the compliment for the whole table. Ken was the quarterback for the Gladiators, the Sweet Valley High football team, and he had thrown the pass that clinched the game. With his blond hair and winning smile, he was also one of the cutest guys in the school.

Jessica felt personally responsible for the cheering squad's brilliant performance at the Big Mesa game that afternoon. Even though she shared the title of cocaptain with Robin Wilson, she considered herself the true team leader. After all, she put more time and energy into the squad than Robin did.

Robin was great at the organizational stuff, like paper work and scheduling practices, but Jessica was the real brains behind the squad. She wrote most of the cheers and choreographed the moves. Still, they were a good team, mainly because there wasn't any rivalry between them. Robin wasn't at all competitive with Jessica. On the contrary, she was just happy to be cocaptain. After all, not so long ago, Robin wasn't even a cheerleader. Jessica remembered the old, chubby Robin Wilson, how she followed Jessica around like a little puppy dog, wanting to be just like her. But now, after recovering from a scary bout with anorexia, where she had gotten much too thin, she looked great and healthy. As far as Jessica was concerned, she was the perfect cocaptain. She helped out just enough, and never stole the limelight.

Like tonight, for instance, Jessica was getting the attention and admiration she felt she deserved. The Dairi Burger was teeming with excitement after the big game. The entire football team was there and dozens of their fans. Everbody was congratulating Jessica on her squad's performance. Nothing made Jessica happier than being in the spotlight—a position she found herself in more often than not.

"I was really proud of all of you today," Jessica said to the cheerleaders as she flipped her hair, aware that she was being watched by a lot of the guys. She felt prettier than ever, and couldn't help noticing that one person in particular had his eye on her: Ken Matthews. Every time she looked up and caught him looking at her, he blushed and looked away.

"I know we've all been working hard in practices, and today our hard work payed off," Jessica said, relishing her role as cocaptain.

"Those new cheers you taught us were great," Annie Whitman said enthusiastically.

"I read about them in *Cheerleading Magazine*," Jessica said with pride. "At first I thought they might be too complicated, but you guys didn't have any problem with them."

"That's because you're such a great teacher," Robin said, smiling.

"Here's to Jessica!" Maria Santelli raised her glass of soda, and all the cheerleaders did the same.

Just as they were about to click their glasses together, Jessica's attention was diverted by a stunning blond girl walking into the Dairi Burger. She apparently wasn't the only one to notice her, as a hush had fallen over the entire room.

"Who's that?" Jessica asked, annoyed that this stranger had interrupted Maria's toast honoring her.

"I don't know, but the guys look like their tongues are about to fall out of their mouths," Lila Fowler teased. "They're practically salivating over her."

Lila, who was Jessica's best friend and at times

her biggest rival, had a knack for saying the exact thing that would make Jessica's blood boil. This was one of those times. *Why can't she just keep her mouth shut?* Jessica wondered.

"She's certainly creating a big stir," Helen Bradley said, as everyone watched the girl make her way over to the take-out counter. "You'd think the entire football team had been hit over the head with a hammer."

"I don't see what all the fuss is about." Jessica scrutinized the girl who was stealing her thunder. "She looks pretty plain if you ask me."

"If that's plain, then in my next life I want to be plain," Jean West said, taking a bite of her sundae. "Check out that body. You probably don't catch her eating sundaes."

"Hey, Winston, put your eyes back in their sockets," Maria said to her boyfriend, Winston Egbert, the class clown, who was sitting on a stool next to the girls' booth.

"Oh, sorry," Winston said with an impish grin. "I was just trying to read what was on her T-shirt."

"Yeah, right," Maria said, shaking her head. "You know, a gorgeous girl walks in the room, and relatively intelligent males are reduced to cavemen in one second."

"Rick Hunter looks like he's about to fall off his stool," Amy Sutton said.

Jessica hardly heard her, though.

"A diet Coke with lemon, please," she heard the girl say, flipping her hair. Then the newcomer gave a dazzling smile to the kid behind the counter. "And I'd like that with a straw."

"Oh, please," Jessica said to her friends, rolling her eyes. "A diet Coke with lemon, please," she mimicked, hair flip and all. "And I'd like that with a straw. Gimme a break."

"That's probably how she stays so thin," Jean said as she watched the girl walk toward the door, sipping her soda.

Everyone in the Dairi Burger seemed to hold their breath as they watched her walk out of the restaurant.

"Whoa mama!" Bruce Patman yelped as the door swung shut behind her.

"Major Babe!" Rick Hunter exclaimed.

Jessica, more annoyed than ever, watched as the girl got into a brand-new white convertible Mazda Miata with "Cheerleader" plates, and revved the engine before she pulled out.

I hope I never lay eyes on that girl again, Jessica thought as she pushed away her hot fudge sundae.

"Slow down, Jess!" Elizabeth said as she braced her hand against the glove compartment of the twins' Jeep on Monday morning. "You're going to have an accident if you don't stop driving like a lunatic."

"Stop worrying so much. It's bad for your

health," Jessica said as she whirled around a corner. "You know I'm an expert driver."

"Since when have you been in such a hurry to get to school?" Usually, Elizabeth had to force her sister to get out of bed, but that morning Jessica was the first one up. "What are you so excited about? Algebra class?"

"Yeah, right." Jessica laughed. "You know I live for algebra." She stopped at a red light and reapplied her matte pink lipstick in the rearview mirror.

"So, what *is* the big rush for?"

"I'm just anxious to get to school because I know everyone's still going to be buzzing about the awesome job we cheerleaders did on Friday—thanks to me, of course," Jessica said excitedly, flooring the gas pedal when the light turned green. "And second of all, I'm looking forward to seeing Ken."

Elizabeth looked out the window at the houses and trees that were whizzing past, so Jessica wouldn't be able to see the pained expression on her face. She wished she could tell her sister what she was feeling, but that was impossible. She couldn't tell her because Jessica didn't know that she had had a fling with Ken when Todd had moved away to Vermont for a brief period earlier that year.

Todd and Ken were best friends, and when Todd was away, he asked Ken to keep an eye on Elizabeth. They spent a lot of time together, and at first they were just good friends. After all, they had known each other since kindergarten. They could talk for hours on end about anything and they had so much in common.

But eventually they realized that their feelings for each other were more than just friendly. Elizabeth had tried to push away her romantic feelings out of loyalty to Todd, but soon she was overcome by her attraction to Ken. When he finally kissed her, she couldn't resist him, and their fling lasted for a couple of weeks.

Finally, though, they decided to end the relationship before anyone—namely Todd—got hurt. The guilt they both felt over deceiving him was destroying them, and they knew it couldn't go on. When Todd came back to Sweet Valley, their relationship had already been over for a long time, and she and Ken had gone back to the way they had always been: just friends. They promised each other to never tell anyone about what had happened while Todd was gone. But because they'd broken off the relationship so quickly—before it had had a chance to cool down naturally—it hadn't really come to a natural end, and now Elizabeth was worried. *Maybe I still have feelings for Ken*, Elizabeth thought as she looked over at her sister's radiant face.

Elizabeth knew better than anyone how horrible it was for Jessica when Jeremy had turned out to be nothing more than a callous criminal, and she wanted to be happy about her sister's new romantic interest, but why did it have to be Ken? The idea of the two of them together drove Elizabeth crazy. *Maybe that kiss they shared on the beach was a fluke*, Elizabeth hoped. *Maybe it will all blow over....*

Where is everyone? Jessica wondered as she stood by her locker on Monday morning. She had been taking her time hanging out in the hallway before going to her first class, wanting to give people a chance to shower her with praise about Friday's game. Normally, her friends swarmed around her on Mondays before first period, eager to talk about the weekend, but nobody seemed to be around. *That's strange,* she thought as she brushed her hair in the little mirror that hung on the inside of her locker door.

That morning, when she'd gotten dressed, she'd been thinking of Ken and wanted to look her very best for him. She decided on her favorite, faded blue jeans and her blue-and-gold gauzy blouse that looked like it was from the sixties. For a minute she wondered if it was her style, but then she decided that since she'd seen blouses like it in all the fashion magazines, it was just right. Besides, blue was a great color on her and she knew she looked beautiful.

She couldn't wait to see Ken again after they'd kissed on Friday night. All weekend she'd played that moment in the moonlight over and over in her head. Just when she was about to give up on romance and guys, she mused, Ken had come along with his gorgeous smile and swept her away.

Just then she heard a buzz of voices down the hallway. She looked toward the commotion and caught a glimpse of Ken at the end of the hall. He was standing in a big crowd of people who were swarming around someone or something. Lila spotted Jessica, and breaking free from the crowd, met her at her locker. "Did you see her yet?"

"Did I see who yet?" Jessica asked, flipping her head over and letting her hair fall back in place to give it more volume. Now that she'd spotted Ken, she wanted to look as good as possible.

"Heather Mallone," Lila said, pointing down the hall to the crowd of people. "That girl at the Dairi Burger on Friday who caused such a big hoopla with the guys."

"What about her?" Jessica said, slamming her locker door. She knew she wasn't going to like whatever Lila was about to tell her, and she already felt the great mood she'd been in that morning start to fade away.

"Well, that's her down there," Lila said. "She just moved to Sweet Valley and she's a student here now. You should see the way the guys are flirting their heads off with her."

"And that's headline news?" Jessica said, trying to sound casual.

"Well," Lila said. "I have a feeling she's going to be pretty popular, judging from the reaction she's getting after just being here a few minutes."

"Whoop-dee-doo," Jessica said, twirling her finger in the air. "Let's call the local television station and tell them the big scoop: A new girl has arrived in Sweet Valley. I mean, who cares?"

"I do. She seems like someone we might want to know. She seems like our type. Oh, and by the way," Lila added casually, looking closely at Jessica, "I think I heard her saying something about being a big deal on her old cheerleading squad."

Jessica knew her best friend well enough to know that Lila was just trying to get a rise out of her.

"As I said in the Dairi Burger," Jessica said, doing her best to smile. "I don't see what the fuss is about. 'Big deal' is a relative term, and besides, she's probably got some major personality flaw."

"How can you possibly know that?" Lila asked as she adjusted the tight purple minidress she was wearing. "You haven't even met her yet. I think I detect a note of jealousy."

"Be real," Jessica said, rolling her eyes. "I can tell things about people from just looking at them." *And major personality flaw or not, I can tell that I don't like anything about this girl*, Jessica thought, mad that for the second time in a row this Heather Mallone had stolen her thunder.

"Here she comes," Lila said.

Jessica turned to watch Heather and a sea of people walk down the hall toward her. She scanned the crowd for Ken, but he wasn't there. Her heart sank for a moment, and then her gaze landed on Heather, who was beaming at her with what Jessica knew was a phony smile.

"Lila, you know Heather, right?" Annie asked.

"Well, we just met a little while ago in the parking lot," Lila said, extending her hand to meet Heather's. "But we weren't properly introduced. I'm Lila Fowler."

"Hi, I'm Heather Mallone. Thanks again for letting me have that parking space."

"No, problem," Lila said. "That's a great car you have, by the way. It's totally cool."

Jessica couldn't believe how Lila was kissing up to Heather. And she let her have her parking space?

"Thanks," Heather said. "I'd be happy to take you riding in it sometime. I'm still unfamiliar with Sweet Valley, and I could use a good tour guide."

"That would be great," Lila said.

I'll be your tour guide, Jessica thought, *I'll show you the way right out of town.*

"This is Jessica Wakefield," Lila said, pushing Jessica forward.

"Hi, Jessica," Heather said smiling that same syrupy smile as she extended her hand to Jessica. "What an adorable little blouse you're wearing. It's so, uh . . . retro."

208

"Retro?" Jessica repeated, not knowing exactly what Heather meant but pretty sure it wasn't a compliment. *I knew I wasn't going to like this person*, Jessica thought as she scrutinized the girl standing in front of her.

Heather had long blond hair that was wavy and curly and hung in layers around her face. She had big blue eyes and a dainty little nose, and as much as Jessica hated to admit it to herself—she *was* beautiful. She was wearing skintight designer blue jeans that showed off a muscular but thin figure, and a white silk blouse that looked tailored and elegant. She had on expensive-looking black loafers with no socks. And her jewelry, which consisted of gold earrings, a gold bracelet, and a gold choker, were from a line Jessica recognized from one of the most exclusive jewelry cataloges she'd seen at Lila's house.

Jessica suddenly knew what Lila meant when she said that Heather was "our type." *She really meant that Heather was her type, as in, super rich!*

"Yeah, you know, 'retro,' like from the sixties," Heather explained authoritatively. "That look is very trendy these days." Jessica looked at Lila, then at Annie, in disbelief. She was waiting for them to acknowledge the fact that Heather was insulting her, but nobody else seemed to notice. *Not only is she a fake, but she's condescending and rude*, Jessica thought.

"Excuse me, but I have to get to class,"

Jessica said as she turned and stormed off. In just a few minutes Jessica's mood had taken a nosedive, and it was all because of one person— Heather Mallone. *The less I see of that girl the better*, Jessica thought as she walked down the hall leaving behind Heather and her group of adoring fans.

The cheerleaders were stretching on the far end of the football field when Jessica arrived at practice on Monday afternoon, and Jessica was excited to start teaching a new cheer she'd worked on all weekend. She quickly read over the cheer she'd written down, and she couldn't wait to share it with the girls.

She dropped her notebook on the ground, feeling proud of the great new words, and ran in front of the waiting squad.

"Okay, girls," Jessica said loudly. "You all did a fantastic job on Friday and I'm not the only one who thinks so. The crowd loved us, and we were better than ever. We can't rest on laurels, though, so I want you to pay close attention to the new routine I'm about to show you."

When Jessica had finished talking, she realized that most of the girls were looking at something behind her. She turned around and saw Heather with her hands on her hips and a smirk on her face.

"May I help you?" Jessica asked, unable to keep the annoyance out of her voice.

"Yeah, as a matter of fact, you can," Heather said. "I want to try out for the squad."

Over my dead body, Jessica wanted to say. But instead she cleared throat and said sweetly, "Well, then, you can come back in the spring and try out with the other seventy-five or so girls that want to be on our squad. Why don't you run along home now and practice, and come back next season."

Jessica turned back toward the girls and raised her arms to start the first cheer.

"Wait, Jessica!" Robin shouted. "I asked Heather to come to practice. I thought that we could really benefit from her expertise, so I invited her to try out. I know it's not really the usual time of year that we audition new people, but I thought we could make an exception since she was the captain of a champion team at her old school."

Jessica could hardly believe her ears. Now she had no choice. Robin was her cocaptain, and if Jessica made a big stink about Heather trying out, everyone would think she was jealous. "Fine, Heather can try out," Jessica said. *But she's going to wish she never came to practice today after I'm through with her.* "I want you to do a triple-herky, a backflip, a Y-leap combination, a no-hands cartwheel, and a landing jump in the splits. Oh, and you'll need to do that in under three minutes."

"No problem," Heather said nonchalantly. "Do you have a watch to time me with?"

"Yes, I do," Jessica said. "On your mark, get set, go!"

Jessica sat down with the other girls, and much to her dismay, watched Heather complete the routine in two minutes. Not only did she do everything Jessica said, but she added complicated, funky dance steps in between each move. When she finished, she gave Jessica one of her sickeningly sweet smiles. Jessica had never seen anyone do such a complicated routine with such expertise and grace, and her head was starting to pound.

Everyone stood up to applaud and cheer, and Jessica was desperate. "Sorry, but that was over three minutes," she lied. "Okay, we've wasted enough time, girls. Let's get down to business."

"Jessica, that was two minutes," Robin protested. "I timed it with my new stopwatch."

"It must not be working," Jessica said dismissively.

"My watch said two minutes, too," said Annie.

"So did mine," Helen said.

"Well, I guess I'll have to get my watch fixed." Jessica was flustered and she felt her face turning red. She looked at Heather, who was as cool as a cucumber. She wasn't even sweating or breathing heavily after that strenuous routine.

"So I think that does it," Robin said. "It looks like we have a new member on the squad."

Has Jessica finally met her match? Find out in **Jessica Quits the Squad,** *the first book in the next three-part miniseries.*

It's Your
First Love. . .
Yours *and* His.

Love Stories

Nobody Forgets
Their First Love!

Now there's a romance series
that gets to the heart of *every-*
one's feelings about falling in
love. *Love Stories* reveals how
boys feel about being in love,
too! In every story, a boy and
girl experience the real-life ups
and downs of being a couple,
and share in the thrills, joys,
and sorrows of first love.

MY FIRST LOVE, Love Stories #1
0-553-56661-X $3.50/$4.50 Can.

SHARING SAM, Love Stories #2
0-553-56660-1 $3.50/$4.50 Can.

Coming in February 1995

Bantam Doubleday Dell
Books For Young Readers   BFYR 104-7/94

Here's an excerpt from
Love Stories #1,

My First Love

THE NIGHT THAT Rick Finnegan kissed me changed my life—but not in the way I'd expected.

He had given me a ride home from my best friend Blythe Carlson's house, where we'd all been drilling one another on vocabulary for the PSATs. There we were, sitting in his dad's Buick outside the Palms bungalow apartments, where my mom and I live, when, out of nowhere, Rick slipped his arm around me.

I don't know what got into him, but one minute he'd been defining the word *alacrity,* and the next thing I knew he was demonstrating it. He moved across the seat so fast that I didn't have time to react. Suddenly his gaping mouth was on mine. Instinctively, I closed my eyes—and he kissed me.

"Amy, I—I think I'm starting to like you," Rick whispered.

My eyes flew open in surprise. But instead of seeing Rick, I saw Chris Shepherd, who's on my swim team, the Dolphins, and who's in my physics class, too. He's also the guy I've been daydreaming about for weeks. "I'm the one you really want," Chris-in-my-mind said. I gasped and jumped away from Rick, leaving him to kiss air where my face had been.

"Rick!" I shrieked, staring at him.

"Amy?" Rick said, looking sheepish. "Are you mad? What's wrong?"

"N-n-nothing," I stuttered, trying to collect my thoughts. I couldn't believe that Rick Finnegan—Mr. Practical and my long time friend—had just kissed me!

I put my hand on his shoulder. "Look, Rick," I said gently. "I'm very flattered. You're a great guy. But we're friends—and I'd like to keep it that way. I don't have time for romance."

But Rick didn't look convinced. "Amy," he said, twisting a lock of my straight blond hair around his finger, "you know what they say about all work and no play. . . ."

"Maybe," I said, stepping out of the car, "but all play and no work gets you a career dipping cones at Dairy Queen."

Actually, I didn't say that. I didn't even think up this perfect comeback until the next day. What came out instead were my mother's words, words often meant for me.

"Your passion is misguided," I informed him, closing the car door behind me.

"My *what*?" I saw Rick's lips form the question behind the window glass right before I waved and turned away.

I couldn't believe I had said that. Mom uses *passion* in a totally different way, as in *enthusiasm for something*. It has nothing to do with feelings for someone. I felt kind of bad saying that, but I didn't know what else would work. Rick and I have known each other since elementary school, and the kiss really caught me off guard. I turned again to go back and apologize, but he was already driving away.

I stood for a minute outside our bungalow apartment, looking up at the stars and thinking about the fact that one of my oldest and best friends had just kissed me. When did Rick's feelings for me change, and why didn't I know about it? I had felt nothing when Rick's lips were on mine. But for some unknown reason, just the thought of Chris Shepherd's lips sent my heart racing. It was true, what I'd said to

219

Rick—I never *had* had time for guys. Until now.

Chris and I had known each other for a couple of years from the swim team, but he had never treated me any differently than any other girl on the team. He was always friendly, and he kidded around, but that was it.

I had always liked Chris, but over the last few months I had been noticing different things about him—admiring his long, lean body; his thick, glossy brown hair; his quick sense of humor . . .

I shook my head to get rid of the thoughts. I had feelings for Chris I'd never had for a guy, but I was still too shy to do anything about it. He had been a fantasy tonight and he'd probably always be a fantasy, I thought dejectedly as I headed inside our bungalow.

"You're just in time for the latest episode of *Search for the Stars*," Mom said as I walked into our combination living/dining room. Mom worked two jobs. She worked from nine to three at the Arizona Bank, and evenings at the El Rancho supermarket. Everyday she taped her favorite soaps, and in the evenings she'd curl up on the couch and watch them.

"Thanks, but I've been studying vocabulary for hours," I told her. "I'm afraid I'll erase what I've learned if I zone out on TV."

"Good for you," Mom said. "You go ahead and get a good night's sleep."

"I think I will." I hesitated for a moment. "Mom? Something pretty weird just happened," I said.

"What?"

"Well . . . Rick drove me home from Blythe's. And . . . he . . . well, he, um . . . told me he liked me," I explained, blushing. I didn't think I needed to tell her about the kiss. It was kind of embarrassing.

Mom sat up straight. "What did you say?"

"I told him I didn't like him that way. That we were just friends." I watched as Mom breathed an almost undetectable sigh of relief.

"Good answer, honey. With your schedule, a boyfriend is the last thing you need," she said.

"Yeah. I guess," I said, shrugging.

I kissed her on the cheek and went to my room. There's no way I could have sat through the soap. I was having a hard enough time putting Chris out of my mind and concentrating on my work. The last thing I needed at the moment was to fill my aching brain with stories about star-crossed lovers and abandoned dreams.

★　　★　　★

The PSAT, it turned out, was a nightmare of words I'd never used and math I'd understood for about an hour in ninth grade. It was bad enough that my brain was fried from choosing among *A, B, C,* or *none of the above,* and that my hand was numb from filling in those tiny circles with a sweat-slick number-two pencil. But the worst part was the reel-to-reel reruns of that kiss that played in my head all day.

And it wasn't Rick's kiss that I kept seeing—that was something we both wanted to forget, I was sure. It was Chris's. I couldn't stop picturing what it would be like to kiss him. In my mind his lips were soft and warm and firm. Then, when his lips found mine, I had that roller-coaster feeling—my heart plunged into my stomach and then began the slow, suspenseful crawl right back up to my chest.

The next thing I knew, I was sighing so loudly that people on both sides of me turned and stared. At the same time the proctor announced, "Fifteen minutes left." What was I *doing*? How could I blow this? Embarrassed and frantic, I raced through the rest of the test.

*   *   *

I was relieved when the PSATs were over, though considering my state of mind when I'd taken it, I was worried about my score. As we left the room, everyone seemed to be talking at once.

"Did you finish the analogy section?"

"How do you find the least common denominator in fractions?"

"Does anyone know what *apposite* means?"

For the rest of the day my honors classes were a chorus of collective anxiety. When my last class was over at three o'clock, I fled to the gym, where I hoped to somehow rinse myself of it all by putting on my racing suit and plunging into the pool before practice.

The rest of the team wasn't due to help put in the lanes for another half hour, so I had the open pool to myself. I love swimming more than anything else in the world. As I stood on the deck and looked at the tranquil water, I began to feel calm. For the next two hours, all I'd have to do would be concentrate on picking up another win in the 200 freestyle this weekend.

I took a few running steps and blasted the water's smooth surface with a cannonball. As always, the water was chilly, so I started swimming warm-ups, steaming back and forth from end to end. Believe me, after two seasons on the swim team, I knew that pool so well that I could swim it in my sleep.

By the fourth lap, I was cruising—when suddenly I crashed into someone and swallowed a mouthful of water.

"Amy, are you alright?" asked a soft male voice as I surfaced, coughing. It was Chris.

"I'm fine," I said, coughing again. I wiped the water dribbling from my mouth off my chin. "I didn't see you."

"I'm sorry," he said. "I saw you swimming laps when I got into the water. I should have gotten out of your way. I know it sounds stupid, but I was just floating on my back and thinking." He looked at me with real concern. "I'm sorry."

"Don't sweat it," I said shyly. "It's just that I thought I had the pool to myself." I wanted to duck my whole face underwater or at least hide my eyes. Could he tell by looking, I wondered, that my mind was spinning constant reruns about kissing him?

Chris returned to floating on his back. His brown hair fanned out like a paintbrush behind him. "If you close your eyes," he said, "you can pretend it's a lake, it's so calm and quiet."

I watched him as he lazily kicked his legs and drifted, eyes closed, toward the middle of the pool. "What are you doing?" I asked.

"I'm watching myself break the regional record for the breaststroke," he explained.

Great, I was thinking, *while I'm picturing kisses, he's imagining fame.* Nervously, I asked, "Do you really think imagining something can make it come true?"

Chris laughed. "I'll know when I reach the finish line."

Even though he looked sort of strange floating there, I admired his quiet determination. Chris is the fastest swimmer on the Dolphins, but breaking the breaststroke record was something that he had never been able to do.

I loved watching him. His body was long and thin, yet muscular. I'm about 5'7" and pretty thin myself, but I don't move as gracefully as Chris.

Several Dolphins came into the pool area then, their voices sending echoes across the floor tiles. Not even this commotion disturbed Chris's concentration. I wondered what part of the race he was mentally swimming just then.

As he drifted nearby, I wanted to reach down and gently stir the water, send it rippling to

225

touch him. Instead I ducked my head back under and continued swimming laps.

I swam freestyle for a few lengths, feeling confident in the water—until I made a graceless flip turn, whacking my heel against the lip of the pool.

"Ouch!" I yelled. I hadn't meant to cause a commotion, but as I limped along the side of the pool to the starting blocks, I could see that Chris was moving toward my lane. My heart skipped a beat when I realized he was waiting for me.

"Your timing's off," he told me when I stopped to get my breath. He touched my wrist, and I was suddenly aware of his long, strong fingers. I stiffened, and he must have noticed, because he took his hand away immediately and let it skim the surface of the pool.

"That's what Coach August says," I said, trying to sound casual, as though my wrist weren't burning from his touch. "He says I turn too late."

"Not too late, exactly, but too cautiously. Your turn would be right on target if you didn't mentally pull back just as you got to the wall. It's like you trip yourself up."

Chris was probably right—it wasn't so much the turn but the dread of it that kept me from swimming full speed. I constantly imagined bashing my heels. And that was exactly what kept happening.

"You could do a neater flip turn and probably shave twenty seconds off your time if you didn't hold back and just charged," Chris said. "Otherwise, it's like you're swimming with your mental brakes on."

"That makes sense," I said. "But how do I charge if I'm terrified I'll hit the lip of the pool?"

"By picturing doing it perfectly so many times that you really believe you can." He waded over to grab a kickboard from the pool deck. "First," he said, tossing me the Styrofoam board, "you've got to relax. Here, float and breathe deeply." He walked over and steadied the board.

But it was hard to relax with Chris staring down at me. I lay there looking up at him. All I could think about were his deep-set brown eyes. There was an intenseness in them, and a kindness as well. I felt like I was about to blush.

"Good so far," Chris said, gently brushing his fingers across my brow. "Now close your eyes."

I squeezed them shut and waited. "Not so

tightly," Chris advised. "What do you see?"

You, I wanted to say. Aloud I said, "I see myself lying on a kickboard, looking stupid, in the middle of the pool."

"Amy, be serious."

"I am." At first I was too self-conscious to imagine anything but the rest of the Dolphins making fun of me. But after a while I got the hang of it. I saw myself in the practice pool, speeding toward the end of the lane. I was surprised that the mental picture was so vivid. "I'm swimming," I said, still feeling kind of silly.

"And?"

"I'm watching the lane lines, getting close to the lip."

"Okay, now try to imagine keeping up your speed. What are you thinking?"

"Don't hit the lip, don't hit it, don't hit it—wham!" I opened my eyes then, and instinctively reached down to rub my heel.

"Try again," Chris said gently.

"What's the use?" I moaned. "I can't do it."

I thought then that he'd give up, but instead he urged me on. "This time, instead of thinking 'don't hit it,' try thinking 'flip.'"

I closed my eyes and was mentally halfway down the lane when I stopped midstroke to ask, "Why?"

"Because your brain takes the 'don't' out of 'don't hit the lip.' And your body only does what your brain tells it to."

If that was true, I was in trouble, because there were plenty of my mother's "don'ts" rattling around in my head. *Don't apologize for your intelligence, don't mope about what you don't have, don't take your education for granted, don't underestimate yourself, don't expect something for nothing, don't throw away your future on some guy.* For years I'd been repeating those commands in my head, maybe dooming myself to do the very things I'd told myself not to.

In my mind I began my stroke again, saying "flip, flip, flip" under my breath, swimming as fast as I could imagine. Then, before I knew it, I'd turned in the water almost effortlessly.

"Hey, I did it!" I said, and opened my eyes in time to see Chris looking at me intently, studying me the way I'd studied him.

Just then Coach August blew his whistle, signaling it was time to put the lanes in for practice. I slid off the kickboard and let myself sink. "Thanks," I said shyly.

"Anytime," Chris said, smiling. Then he turned away and swam toward the coach.

Anytime, I thought happily as I dove underwater.

Anytime . . .

I was the last one to leave the girls' locker room after practice that afternoon, mostly because I was thinking so much about Chris that I couldn't get moving. As I walked out of school, he was sitting in the grass by my bus stop.

I was surprised. He lived on the east side of town, and I lived on the west. "Hey, Chris," I called out as I crossed the street. "Aren't you waiting for the wrong bus?"

"I was waiting for you," he said.

I thought my heart would stop. "Me?" I managed to say.

He smiled as he stood up and brushed the grass off his faded, torn Levi's. "Yeah," he said. "I thought you might want a ride home."

"You've got a car?"

He pointed in the direction of the school parking lot behind me. "It's my brother Dave's. It's that sixty-four Mustang," he said. "Dave said I could use it today. He's home on break from college."

I turned and saw this gleaming classic car. I knew that Chris came from a pretty wealthy family, but because he always wore Levi's with holes in the knees, T-shirts, and baseball caps, I had never thought about it. "Cool," I said as we walked toward the convertible, trying to conceal the excitement I felt.

Chris opened the car door, and I got in. As he slipped into the driver's side, I glanced at him out of the corner of my eye. Just the night before, I had been in Rick's car, being kissed by him and seeing Chris. Now I was actually in a car with Chris! Maybe thinking about things really could make them happen.

Bantam Books in the Sweet Valley High series
Ask your bookseller for the books you have missed

#1 DOUBLE LOVE

#2 SECRETS

#3 PLAYING WITH FIRE

#4 POWER PLAY

#5 ALL NIGHT LONG

#6 DANGEROUS LOVE

#7 DEAR SISTER

#8 HEARTBREAKER

#9 RACING HEARTS

#10 WRONG KIND OF GIRL

#11 TOO GOOD TO BE TRUE

#12 WHEN LOVE DIES

#13 KIDNAPPED!

#14 DECEPTIONS

#15 PROMISES

#16 RAGS TO RICHES

#17 LOVE LETTERS

#18 HEAD OVER HEELS

#19 SHOWDOWN

#20 CRASH LANDING!

#21 RUNAWAY

#22 TOO MUCH IN LOVE

#23 SAY GOODBYE

#24 MEMORIES

#25 NOWHERE TO RUN

#26 HOSTAGE

#27 LOVESTRUCK

#28 ALONE IN THE CROWD

#29 BITTER RIVALS

#30 JEALOUS LIES

#31 TAKING SIDES

#32 THE NEW JESSICA

#33 STARTING OVER

#34 FORBIDDEN LOVE

#35 OUT OF CONTROL

#36 LAST CHANCE

#37 RUMORS

#38 LEAVING HOME

#39 SECRET ADMIRER

#40 ON THE EDGE

#41 OUTCAST

#42 CAUGHT IN THE MIDDLE

#43 HARD CHOICES

#44 PRETENSES

#45 FAMILY SECRETS

#46 DECISIONS

#47 TROUBLEMAKER

#48 SLAM BOOK FEVER

#49 PLAYING FOR KEEPS

#50 OUT OF REACH

#51 AGAINST THE ODDS

#52 WHITE LIES

#53 SECOND CHANCE

#54 TWO-BOY WEEKEND

#55 PERFECT SHOT

#56 LOST AT SEA

#57 TEACHER CRUSH

#58 BROKENHEARTED

#59 IN LOVE AGAIN

#60 THAT FATAL NIGHT

#61 BOY TROUBLE

#62 WHO'S WHO?

#63 THE NEW ELIZABETH

#64 THE GHOST OF TRICIA MARTIN

#65 TROUBLE AT HOME

#66 WHO'S TO BLAME?

#67 THE PARENT PLOT

#68 THE LOVE BET

#69 FRIEND AGAINST FRIEND

#70 MS. QUARTERBACK

#71 STARRING JESSICA!

#72 ROCK STAR'S GIRL

#73 REGINA'S LEGACY

#74 THE PERFECT GIRL

#75 AMY'S TRUE LOVE

#76 MISS TEEN SWEET VALLEY

#77 CHEATING TO WIN

#78 THE DATING GAME

#79 THE LONG-LOST BROTHER

#80 THE GIRL THEY BOTH LOVED

#81 ROSA'S LIE

#82 KIDNAPPED BY THE CULT!

#83 STEVEN'S BRIDE

#84 THE STOLEN DIARY

#85 SOAP STAR

#86 JESSICA AGAINST BRUCE

#87 MY BEST FRIEND'S BOYFRIEND

#88 LOVE LETTERS FOR SALE

#89 ELIZABETH BETRAYED

#90 DON'T GO HOME WITH JOHN

#91 IN LOVE WITH A PRINCE

#92 SHE'S NOT WHAT SHE
    SEEMS

#93 STEPSISTERS

#04 ARE WE IN LOVE?

#95 THE MORNING AFTER

#96 THE ARREST

#97 THE VERDICT

#98 THE WEDDING

#99 BEWARE THE BABY-SITTER

#100 THE EVIL TWIN (MAGNA)

#101 THE BOYFRIEND WAR

#102 ALMOST MARRIED

#103 OPERATION LOVE MATCH

#104 LOVE AND DEATH IN
     LONDON

#105 A DATE WITH A WEREWOLF

#106 BEWARE THE WOLFMAN
     (SUPER THRILLER)

#107 JESSICA'S SECRET LOVE

#108 LEFT AT THE ALTAR

#109 DOUBLE-CROSSED

#110 DEATH THREAT

#111 A DEADLY CHRISTMAS
     (SUPER THRILLER)

SUPER EDITIONS:
    PERFECT SUMMER
    SPECIAL CHRISTMAS
    SPRING BREAK
    MALIBU SUMMER
    WINTER CARNIVAL
    SPRING FEVER

SUPER STARS:
    LILA'S STORY
    BRUCE'S STORY
    ENID'S STORY
    OLIVIA'S STORY
    TODD'S STORY

SUPER THRILLERS:
    DOUBLE JEOPARDY
    ON THE RUN
    NO PLACE TO HIDE
    DEADLY SUMMER
    MURDER ON THE LINE
    BEWARE THE WOLFMAN
    A DEADLY CHRISTMAS

MAGNA EDITIONS:
    THE WAKEFIELDS OF
        SWEET VALLEY
    THE WAKEFIELD LEGACY:
        THE UNTOLD STORY
    A NIGHT TO REMEMBER
    THE EVIL TWIN
    ELIZABETH'S SECRET DIARY
    JESSICA'S SECRET DIARY

SIGN UP FOR THE SWEET VALLEY HIGH® FAN CLUB!